deadly silence

Lex broke into a run, darting from one clump of thick brush to the next, zigzagging over the open ground and keeping his eyes on the wickiups. There was no sign of life—no horses, no barking dogs, nothing. He picked up his pace, trying to push from his mind the thought that whatever had happened here, he was too late to do anything about it.

He nearly stumbled over the first body, all but hidden by thick brush, just one leg jutting out into the open. He knew immediately that it had to be a child. The leg was so thin, the legginged foot so tiny. He knelt and reached into the brush to push it aside. He saw the face then, but couldn't tell whether it was a boy or girl.

The scalp was gone.

Also by
Dan Mason

The Ranger
Border Bandits
Comanche Raiders
Range War
Track Down

**Published by
HarperPaperbacks**

DAN MASON

THE RANGER

APACHE THUNDER®

HarperPaperbacks
A Division of HarperCollinsPublishers

This is a work of fiction. The characters, incidents, and dialogues are products of the author's imagination and are not to be construed as real. Any resemblance to actual events or persons, living or dead, is entirely coincidental.

HarperPaperbacks   *A Division of* HarperCollins*Publishers*
10 East 53rd Street, New York, N.Y. 10022

Cover illustration by Larry Schwinger

First printing: July 1992

Printed in the United States of America

HarperPaperbacks and colophon are trademarks of HarperCollins*Publishers*

❖ 10 9 8 7 6 5 4 3 2 1

WADE DALTREY scooped beans from a tin plate, ignoring the grease accumulating on his beard as he shoveled the food into his mouth. He looked at the half-dozen men arrayed around the fire and shook his head.

Tim Culver noticed the gesture. "Something wrong, Wade?" he asked.

Daltrey shook his head again, this time more forcefully. "Nope."

"The hell there ain't," Culver insisted. "What's eatin' at you? You ain't been right for three, four weeks, now. Seems like somethin's on your mind."

"If I got somethin' to say, Timmy, I'll say it. Just shut up and lemme eat."

"Wade needs a woman." Ralph Gleason said. "Ain't that right, Wade?"

Daltrey snorted, but kept on eating. In the firelight, the deep creases in his sun-bronzed skin were full of shadows. His black hair, greasy and tangled, hung to his shoulders and drooped over his forehead. His thick hands made the tin plate look frail as he cradled it on his fingers and dabbed the age-stiffened bread into the bean juice.

His eyes, black as two lumps of coal, glittered in the orange light that made them look like small obsidian globes full of fireflies. Stuffing the last of the bread into his mouth, he tossed the plate to one side and turned his gaze on Gleason.

"Now I'm done eatin', Ralph. You want to say that again?"

Gleason shook his head. "Just jokin' with you, Wade. That's all. I didn't mean nothing by it."

"You don't mean nothing, you shouldn't say nothing."

Gleason bobbed his head and swallowed hard. He'd seen Daltrey like this before. They all had. And it always meant trouble. "I know it," Gleason said. "I know that. Sorry, Wade."

Daltrey nodded slowly, then stood up. At six two, and a good two hundred and twenty pounds, he towered over the small circle of men around the fire. "I know you didn't mean nothing," Ralph," he said. He stepped toward the fire then, like a snake that had suddenly made up its mind to strike, his right leg lashed out and the toe of his boot caught Gleason under the chin.

A sound like that of a thick twig snapping echoed off the rocky butte behind Daltrey as Gleason fell backward. He lay there for a moment, Daltrey watching. The big man stepped across the fire then, ignoring the heat of the flames as he squatted beside the prostrate Gleason. "Next time you don't mean nothing, I bet you don't say nothing either."

Gleason groaned, and tried to sit up. Blood ran down over his chin, and he shook his head before spitting. More blood and water spewed into the dirt, where the nubs of two teeth gleamed whitely in the sticky pool. Daltrey stood again and rubbed the greasy hair of his beard, looked at his hand, then wiped the fingers on his pants.

"No call to do Ralph that way, Wade," Culver said.

Daltrey spun around and made as if to kick Culver, then lowered his foot to the ground and laughed. "Didn't mean nothing, Timmy," he said, then laughed again.

Everybody but Gleason laughed. The latter tried to smile, but his face just twisted into a grimace. He wiped idly at the blood on his chin, grabbed a handful of dust, and clapped his hands together.

"I'm gettin' pretty tired of this shit," Daltrey said then. "Seems like I run halfway across the country and back with you bastards and I got nothin' to show for it. I'd like to make some real money for a change."

Culver nodded. "I knew there was something bothering you."

"Timmy, you ain't known for your thinkin', so maybe you should just shut up."

"Whatever you say, Wade."

"I'll tell you what. Tomorrow, first thing, we're gonna head out and get us some new horses, then we're gonna see can we make us some money. Real money."

"Where we going to get horses?" The questioner was Pete Carmody, and he looked at Daltrey with his head cocked to one side. "Seems like we been following you from here to hell and back and got nothing to show for it."

"You want to leave, Pete?" Daltrey asked.

"Maybe I do."

"Fine. Then you pack up and git. I don't need nobody who don't want to be here."

"All right. I'll leave first thing in the morning."

"Wrong, Pete. You'll leave right now. Go on, git." Daltrey took a step toward Carmody, who rolled to one side then sprang to his feet.

"Whatever you say, Wade." Carmody walked toward his horse, stooped to scoop up his saddle and saddle blanket, and flipped the blanket onto his horse's back.

Hoisting the saddle, he had it poised over the blanket when Daltrey said, "Pete?"

Carmody turned and saw Daltrey walking toward him. "I changed my mind," the big man said. "You ain't goin' nowhere."

Carmody shook his head. He clicked his tongue against his teeth, and lowered the saddle to the horse. "I think maybe I should, Wade," he said. "Probably not a good idea for me to stay."

"Oh," Daltrey said, "I don't want you to stay."

"But I thought you..."

"I just don't want you to go," Daltrey interrupted. He pulled his Colt and stuck it in Carmody's gut. The cowboy started to back up, but Daltrey bored in with the barrel of the pistol. Carmody started to twist away as Daltrey pulled the trigger.

The bullet passed through the cowboy just under the ribs and passed out the man's back just above the hip, splattering the horse with blood.

Carmody slumped to the ground and Daltrey leaned over him. "I think he's still alive," he said. He thumbed back the hammer on his Colt, pressed the muzzle against Carmody's forehead, and fired again. Tucking the gun in his holster, he turned back toward the fire. "That's one less horse we need," he grunted. "Now, anybody else want to quit on me?"

Daltrey surveyed the faces of the men around the fire. None of them said anything, and one by one they turned their eyes away to stare into the fire or examine the ground between their outstretched feet. None looked in Carmody's direction.

"Good," Daltrey said, then turned to the horse and yanked the saddle off, letting it fall to the ground. Walking back to the fire, he said, "Timmy, drag him off a ways and throw some dirt over him. He'll start to stink before too long."

Lowering himself to the ground, Daltrey scraped a callused hand across his chin. He lay back then, tilted his hat forward and stared at the men from under its brim. One by one, they curled up on the ground, pulled their blankets over them, and went to sleep.

Daltrey lay there listening to the scrape of Carmody's boots on the ground as Culver dragged him off into the darkness. Culver returned for an entrenching tool, glanced at Daltrey, then disappeared into the darkness again. Daltrey sat up and opened the saddlebags he was using as a pillow, pulled out a bottle of whiskey, and opened it.

The big man drank quietly, letting the rotgut sear him on its way down. Sipping slowly, he downed a quarter of the bottle, then tilted it back and took a long pull, choked it down, and capped the bottle again, stuffed it into the saddlebags once more, and lay down.

He felt his stomach twisting in knots and knew it wasn't from the whiskey. He just felt like things were out of control, like he had to do something to feel good about himself again. He was tired of nickel-and dime-pillage. It was time for a big score, time to put some real money together. But how to do it was the problem. There were a few banks out here in West Texas, but they wouldn't have much in the way of deposits, and it was risky besides.

What he really wanted was some way to fatten his wallet with very little risk. But first things first. And that had to be horses. It didn't much matter what he did next, but he couldn't do anything at all without the horses. If the law got on his trail, the played-out nags he and his men were riding now wouldn't get them very far. Ripsaw was just thirty miles away, El Paso twice as far or a little more, and there were bound to be plenty of horses for the taking. Mostly small spreads, with small crews, if any. They'd be ripe pickings.

He was still lying there, staring out from under his hat, when the sky started to brighten. There was no point in trying to sleep now, so he got up and walked away from the fire, now just smoking embers, and relieved his bladder in a clump of brush.

By the time the sun came up, he had already saddled his mount. He walked back to the fire and sat on the ground, staring at the sleeping men. A bunch of third-rate losers, he thought, men who couldn't think for themselves, and didn't have the courage to strike out on their own. He knew it, and knew that was why they followed him, but the thought made him feel good about himself.

It was satisfying giving orders. He'd done it during the war, and found it came easy. And he'd learned, too, that it didn't matter how well thought out those orders were, as long as they were delivered with authority. Most men would do what you said if they were convinced you knew what you were doing—or if they knew you'd shoot them if they didn't. And Wade Daltrey had killed his share of men.

Carmody was just the latest, an object lesson for the rest of them, a lesson that hadn't been lost on them. At six thirty Daltrey got to his feet, and walked around the camp kicking the soles of the boots, barking "Get up, you lazy bastards. Get up. It's time to ride."

The men moved quickly, stealing glances at the big man as if afraid to look directly at him, fearful he might find some reason to give them the same treatment he'd given Pete Carmody. But Daltrey seemed to be in some kind of fog. He climbed into the saddle and sat there motionless, as if he were posing for one of the countless statues of Stonewall Jackson that were springing up all across the South.

Tim Culver called to him once, but when Daltrey didn't respond right away, he thought it best not to push his luck. The men saddled their horses quickly, grumbling to themselves, but Daltrey seemed not to hear the complaints or, if he did, not to care.

When they were ready, Daltrey turned in the saddle to yell over his shoulder. "We're gonna have a hard ride today, and the next. If we have to, we are gonna rip this part of Texas wide open until we find what we're looking for. Anybody ain't got the stomach for it, be a good idea if he lit out now. Ain't nobody gonna leave once we start."

"Where we goin', Wade?" Culver asked.

"Wherever we feel like, Timmy," Daltrey said, flashing him a wide grin. "Maybe knock over a stage, rob a bank, a train. I don't know and I don't care. Hell, things get real interesting, maybe we'll take some Injun scalps and peddle 'em to the Mexicans." He laughed again.

Culver looked skeptical. "Ain't no money in that, Wade."

"There is, you get enough hair, Timmy. It all depends. You might say it's fate. Whatever happens, that's what's meant to happen." He looked up at the sky then, as if trying to read his own fate on the bottom of a passing cloud. The men waited patiently. Finally, he lowered his eyes to his men once more.

"Let's move," he said.

LEX CRANSHAW clicked home the cylinder of his Colt revolver, tested the weight of the pistol in his hand, and then sighted at the fence rail some fifty feet away. An array of glass bottles, their dark brown made amber by the bright sun, lined the rail like spectators at a rodeo.

Aiming at the first bottle on the left, he squeezed the trigger gently, and felt the heft of the Colt bucking in his hand at the same instant the bottle exploded into a myriad of glittering shards. One by one he worked his way down the rail, knocking off bottle after bottle, until six were gone.

He shook his head unhappily, broke the Colt open, and reloaded. There were plenty of bottles left on the fence, and he meant to knock them all off before he was done. Behind him, the summer camp of Company F, Texas Rangers, was quiet. Most of the men were scattered to the four corners of the state. As usual there were budget problems, and F was, for the moment, the only Company funded by the legislature.

Lex enjoyed the quiet, and spent the time practicing with his new Colt, reading law, and trying to find some way to come to terms with his life. That hadn't been easy for a long, long time. He managed, but just barely, and there was always a little voice echoing deep in his skull that tried to convince him that he was wasting his life.

Maybe he was, he would say, but it's the only way I know how to live right now. I'll change when I'm ready. And when I'm able. But he was not ready yet, and he sure as hell wasn't able. Since his young wife had died in childbirth, his only real solace had been found in solitude and movement. And being a Texas Ranger gave him plenty of both. It was, he knew, the perfect job for the imperfect man Rosalita's death had made of him.

And bang . . . bang . . . bang. Three more bottles blown to hell. The sound of the Colt drowned out the internal voice nagging him. Bang . . . bang . . . bang. And the cylinder was empty once more.

Breaking the Colt open again, he clapped the cylinder full of empties against his palm, ignoring the chime-like tinkle of the shells as they tumbled onto the pile of cartridge casings at his feet. Methodically he yanked live rounds from his gunbelt, hefting the surprising weight of each in his palm for a moment before ramming it home with a dull click.

A few more bottles, and it would be time to call it a day. He was uncomfortable with the new pistol, and wanted to get used to it before he might have to use it. The action was a little stiff, and it seemed to him that the hammer was a bit high. His thumb kept missing when he'd reach to cock the pistol. Looking at it, he tried to remember the contours of his last revolver, wondering whether there was a difference.

Then, with a shrug, he resolved to take the hammer down a bit with a file. It was important to feel right, important that the thumb and the hammer fit like a hand in a well-worn glove. It could make the difference between living and dying, and that was a difference he was determined to have in his favor.

Twice more he emptied the Colt, leaving just two bottles on the fence. After debating with himself whether to shoot them off, he bent over, snatched a rock the size of his fist off the ground, and chucked it toward the fence. It missed both bottles, but struck the top rail with enough force to dislodge them both. They landed in the sand with dull clunks, and lay there in the shade of the fence post, the amber reduced to brown night once more.

Reloading the Colt one last time, he slid it into his holster, and started back to his bunkhouse. He was the only Ranger in camp at the moment, and he wanted to make the most of it. Entering the rough-timbered cabin, he walked to his bunk, unbuckled his gunbelt, and draped it over a chair, then lay down on the cot.

His books were on a wooden shelf just overhead, and he reached up for one without looking. At the moment, he wanted the comfort of words. Whose they were didn't matter. All he needed was to hear them inside his skull, distracting him from his own thoughts. That was all the comfort he'd had in years, and all he'd come to expect.

Cracking the book open, he crooked his knees and let the book rest against his canted thighs. It was a novel, one he'd picked up in Austin the last time he'd been to the capital: *Moby Dick*. He'd never heard of the author, but those were sometimes the best books. The absence of expectations let the book speak for itself. You were ready for it or you weren't.

The sound of hoofbeats distracted him before he found the first page. It was probably his new commanding officer, Schuyler Bradshaw, who'd been assigned to the command three weeks before when Major Earl Podell finally decided he wanted to spend a little time with his family before his kids got too old to know who he was.

Major Bradshaw was cut from the same cloth as Podell. No nonsense, but no spit and polish either. Both men had seen combat during the war, and they knew that it was respect that mattered, not how shiny you kept your shoes. Lex put the book back on the shelf and swung his legs over the edge of the cot. As he stood up, he heard the approaching horse nicker, then skid to a halt.

Lex grabbed his gunbelt and buckled it on as he made for the door. One thing Bradshaw insisted on, and no one had had to tell Lex twice, that his men keep their guns within easy reach. The Rangers were hated by a few as much as they were admired by many, and more than one camp had been attacked by outlaws with a little too much whiskey under their belts and as much time on their hands.

Lex opened the door just as Bradshaw swung out of the saddle in front of his cabin. Stepping outside, Lex felt the heat hit him again, and glanced up at the unforgiving Texas sun. It must have been almost a hundred degrees until nearly four o'clock. Now, with the sun slipping down in the west, it was probably only ninety, but after the shade of the cabin, the heat made its presence felt.

Bradshaw looped the reins over the rickety hitching post in front of his cabin and turned as he heard Lex approaching.

"Cranshaw, how are you?" he asked, as Lex walked across the compound clearing.

"Not bad, Major. Yourself?"

"I been better, Lex. A whole hell of a lot better. I'll tell you that much."

"Anything wrong?"

"When ain't there?"

Lex laughed, and Bradshaw permitted himself a squeeze of his facial muscles that turned into something halfway between a grin and a scowl.

"You know West Texas at all, Lex?"

"Been there three or four times. Why?"

"You're goin' again, is why."

"What's going on?"

"Ever hear of a man named Wade Daltrey?"

Lex nodded. Few Texans hadn't heard of Daltrey. "Yeah."

"What do you know about him?"

"I know that he's trouble. I know that he's killed a dozen men, at least, and probably three times that, if you believe half the stories you hear."

"You can believe 'em. Come on inside. I'll tell you what I know. Then the rest'll be up to you."

Bradshaw unlaced the saddlebags from the back of his mount, draped them over his shoulder, and led the way into his cabin. "Christ on a crutch," he muttered, "It's hotter'n hell in here. Should build a fire to cool it off."

He dumped the saddlebags onto a rude wooden table, then pulled a match from his shirt pocket. Striking it with his thumb, he lifted the chimney of a coal oil lamp, touched the match to the wick until the flame spurted up, then waited until it died down again and kept on flickering, before shaking the match out.

He lowered the chimney into place, adjusted the wick, and opened the saddlebags. One pouch was crammed with papers, some bearing the state seal and others little more than rude notes made with a thick-leaded carpenter's pencil in Bradshaw's neat hand.

"Pull up a chair," the major said, kicking one into place and lowering himself down without looking. Lex followed suit across the table from his commander, and folded his hands on the table-top to wait while Bradshaw rummaged through the papers.

"Here it is," Bradshaw mumbled. "Here's what I'm looking for." He opened an envelope, withdrew two sheets of paper, and read them over, his lips moving to shape the words Lex could almost, but not quite, hear. When he was done, he shoved the paper across the table. "You can look at this later," he said. "Fact, you can bring it with you."

Lex glanced at the two pages before folding them and tucking them into his shirt pocket.

"What do you know about Daltrey?" Bradshaw asked, taking a hand-rolled cigarette out of his pocket along with a second match.

"About the same as everybody else, I guess," Lex said. "He was a cavalry commander during the war—irregulars, like Quantrill, but not nearly as well known. Not as good, either, from what I hear."

"You were in the war, weren't you, Lex?"

Cranshaw nodded. "Yeah, I was."

"Ever run across him?"

Lex shook his head. "Nope. I knew a couple people who'd run into him. That's about it."

"Mean as a snake, he is. I met him once, before his court-martial. Should have hung the bastard is what we shoulda done. Missed a good bet there, all right. Quantrill's a good comparison, I guess, but he's a military genius alongside Mr. Daltrey. Not to mention a saint. And Quantrill's gone to his reward, whatever that might be. I can guess, and I'll bet it's a lot hotter than this damn cabin. Unfortunately, Daltrey's still with us."

"I gather Daltrey has something to do with my assignment?"

"Everything, Lex. He's been tearing across most of West Texas, from the southern panhandle all the way to El Paso for near ten years now. Mostly it's small-time stuff. Robs a bank now and then, or a train. But mostly it's been terrorizin' innocent folks for food, water, and horses. There ain't a lot out there—fit for the devil, really—but Daltrey ain't fit for much else, so I guess you might say he knows his limits. Until recently, nobody much cared, as long as the trouble was small time."

"That's changed, I gather?"

Bradshaw nodded vigorously. "You bet it has. He made the big mistake of raiding a ranch belonged to a cousin of the governor."

"Belonged?"

"He's dead. Daltrey shot him and two hands in cold blood. And he seems to be raiding everyplace, like he's got some big ideas, or something. Nobody can figure what he's up to, but everybody, and by that I mean the governor, wants him stopped. You're the only man I got. I hate to send you alone, but I got no choice."

When Lex didn't answer, Bradshaw looked at him closely. "You can tell me no, if you want to. I'll understand. It's not the . . ."

"No," Lex interrupted. "I'll go."

"I figured you would. Everything we know is in that letter I give you. Read it over tonight. I think you should wait till morning before you head out. You want to know anything else, we'll talk some more then."

LEX HAD been riding for three days. Every night, after pitching camp and having dinner, he read through the two-page letter Major Bradshaw had given to him, and every night he put it away, still not knowing any more than he had when he began his journey.

Distilled to its essence, the letter was little more than an inventory of crimes, real and suspected, for which Wade Daltrey was wanted. The letter had come from a U.S. marshal in El Paso, a man by the name of Walter Perkins, and asked for help in apprehending Daltrey.

The people in the western end of Texas, it seemed, were members of either of two camps: those who wanted to hunt Daltrey and his men down like wolves, and those who were too frightened of the man even to think about seeing him brought to justice. What troubled Lex was that it wasn't clear which camp Perkins slept in.

On the morning of the fourth day he had less than a hundred miles to ride, and was determined to make it by sundown. He rose early and rode hard, knowing that he was already within Daltrey's area of activity, and that he might stumble across the bandits at any time.

According to Perkins, they liked to patrol the roads, and had robbed the stage more than once. Unwary travelers were easy pickings, and Daltrey was more interested in fattening his wallet than he was in demonstrating the bravery that had won him three commendations and several citations from Jefferson Davis during the war.

But Lex knew the war could do strange things to a man. Some came out better men than they had been going in, and some discovered a brutality they hadn't realized existed somewhere deep inside them. But if there was one thing certain, it was that no one had come through unchanged. The war had made itself felt by each and every man who had had the misfortune to come within its greedy reach.

Wade Daltrey, it seemed, was one of those who'd made a wrong turn. Maybe it had been too easy to kill, and he discovered he had a taste for blood. Or maybe Daltrey had been one of those who had to kill the best part of himself in order to survive, to do the job the South demanded of him. Either way, though, it was clear that bringing Daltrey in would not be easy, if it could be done at all.

As he rode, Lex thought back to his own experience of the war and, as he always did, found himself concentrating on, even reliving, the nightmare of Shiloh. He could still smell the blood and the stink of the mud after several days of rain had turned the plowed fields into quagmires. He had been wounded, and if it hadn't been for the kindness of a woman who had no reason at all to care whether he lived or died, he wouldn't have made it.

A former slave, she had taken him in after her young son found him lying in water nearly covering his face, hidden from the road at the edge of a field by weeds thigh high, and matted by the rain. He had lost a lot of blood and was too weak even to turn over when the boy had knelt beside him to see if he were still alive.

That had been more than ten years before, and he could still smell the stench of the killing fields, see the pall of gunsmoke that hung in the damp air like low-lying clouds, and hear the sound of the guns' distant thunder in his ears that made the ground tremble beneath him and sent ripples slapping across the surface of the water in which he lay.

He never did learn her last name. "Miss Emma" was all he'd learned. And that's how he remembered her. She'd been killed by a minié ball a week after dragging him home by brute strength, the boy doing his best to hold Lex by the legs, but dropping them every few steps. Each time his feet hit the ground, the impact sent a shock through the wounded man's body and provoked from the woman a stream of curses that would have done a drill sergeant proud.

As he had lain there in her rude shack, slowly getting his strength back, it had made him wonder whether he had chosen to fight for the wrong side. He still didn't know, but it had taught him two things: nothing is as simple as it seems, and war is simpler than it ought to be.

In mid-afternoon, his eyes aching from squinting into the sun, he stopped for a swig of water, growing nervous about how little was left in his canteen. When he'd wet his parched throat and rinsed some of the trail dust out of his mouth, he shielded his eyes with one hand, holding the canteen in the other and wondering whether he could risk another swig.

He searched the horizon, hoping to spot some trees that would tell him fresh water was nearby, but all he saw was a thin cone of black smoke. As near as he could tell, the fire was a good six or seven miles away, and seemed to be almost dead ahead. He wasn't far from the stage road to El Paso, and wondered if the fire could be coming from a way station.

Capping the canteen, he draped it over the pommel of his saddle and clucked to the big chestnut beneath him. The tired horse was reluctant to respond, but Lex nudged him until he started to move. Then, as if realizing that the man on his back was anxious to get somewhere, he broke into a trot on his own. Lex leaned over to pat the chestnut on its shoulder and whisper encouragement into its ear.

As he drew closer, he noticed that the smoke was starting to thin, as if whatever was burning had been burning for a while. Lex knew there was a chance he was getting anxious about nothing. For all he knew, some farmer might be burning off a field, or trying to burn out a tree stump.

There were a dozen possibilities, most of them perfectly innocent, but it wouldn't hurt to take a look, especially since it wouldn't take him much out of the way.

When he was less than two miles away, the smoke had dwindled down to a wavering wisp. It rose up and fanned out until it was more like isolated puffs than the column he had first seen. Reaching into his saddlebags for binoculars, he trained them on the base of the smoke, but the brilliant sun and shimmering heat blurred everything close to the ground.

He noticed what appeared to be the tops of a few trees, which made him suspect it was either a homestead or a stage way station, but he'd have to get a lot closer before he would know for sure, even with the field glasses.

Draping the glasses around his neck, he urged the chestnut to move a little faster. It had been a long ride, and he wasn't about to push the horse too hard, but his curiosity was aroused now. After he'd gone another mile, he tried with the glasses once more. This time, he was able to make out the blurred outline of several low buildings, but still couldn't tell what they were.

The smoke had died away almost completely now, and he was wondering whether he had gotten concerned about nothing. Then, realizing how tired and thirsty he was, and how much the chestnut needed a rest, he decided it was just as well. He could lay over for an hour or two and, if he was lucky, maybe even get something to eat beside beans and salt pork.

He started to relax, letting the horse set its own pace. He still watched the last wisps of smoke drifting away, but it was more for something to do than anything else. His eyes burned, and it helped to keep them focused on something other than the shimmering horizon.

At half a mile, he changed his mind. The last few puffs of smoke were barely visible, but there was no doubt they had come from the ruins of a building. He could see the stark finger of a stone chimney jabbing up at the smoke as if making an accusation. He spurred the chestnut then, and leaned forward in the saddle, intent now on watching the remains of the building. He had been right about the other buildings. They were sheds and what was probably a corral.

He saw a stage coach beyond the forlorn chimney, the team still hitched, but there seemed to be no one around. Closing on the dying fire, he loosened his Colt in its holster, almost without thinking, then leaned forward to pull a Winchester Model 73 from his saddle boot. Jerking the reins, he slid out of the saddle even before the chestnut had stopped moving.

Running toward the stage, he called, "Hello! Anybody there?"

The only answer was a nicker from one of the sheds, and he glanced toward it while sprinting to the stagecoach. One door of the coach hung open, and seemed to have been sprung from its hinges. As he got closer, he saw three or four bullet holes in the side of the stage.

Once more, he called out, "Anybody here?"

Again there was no answer. He reached the stage and stopped, holding the Winchester waist high as he peered around the door. Two men, both covered with blood, were sprawled in the stage, half on the seats and half on the floor.

Leaning inside, he knew they were dead, and had been for a couple of hours, at least. In the baking heat, it didn't take long for the stench of death to take hold.

Instinctively he glanced at the sky. As he'd expected, two black specks circled high overhead, almost shapeless in the glare. Even as he watched, they dropped lower, their wings barely moving as they rode the hot air currents.

Moving around to the other side of the stage, he found several more bullet holes in the door and the body of the coach. He climbed up to the seat, but there was no sign of anyone. No bloodstains, and no body. Where in hell was the driver, he wondered.

And, more to the point, who had done this?

He walked toward the chimney, just as the last couple of timbers from the burned out station collapsed into the ashes. They sent a shower of sparks arcing out over the ashes, and the breeze kicked up by the collapse uncovered embers that glowed dark red under a thin layer of gray flakes.

Standing beside the chimney, he stared at the ruins, then spotted what he was afraid of seeing. He leaned out over the embers, and felt the heat swat at his cheeks and the exposed skin of his neck. Sweat dripped out from under the brim of his hat and ran into his eyes, making them burn, and he wiped the sleeve of his shirt across them, then blinked away the sting.

Leaning his Winchester against the chimney, he backed away, then turned to the corral. A stack of split rails lay against one wall, and he ran toward it, grabbed the longest, and lugged it back to the ruined way station.

He swung the rail by one end, leaned out over the ashes once more, this time tilting his head to one side, and let the end of the rail crash into the ashes.

Using it like a probe, he turned some of the charred wreckage over and jabbed the rail into a suspicious mound. It moved easily, and as some charred wood fell to one side, he found himself staring at a ribcage, looking for all the world like the frame of a woven basket, almost inhuman as it lay there in the ruins.

Shaking his head, he let the rail fall, and it kicked up a plume of ash and dust. Turning away, he retrieved the Winchester and walked back to the corral.

Once more, he called out. "Anybody here? Hello?"

Still no answer. He searched the buildings one by one, careful not to expose himself in the doorway until he was certain no one was inside. It wouldn't do to have some frightened stage driver take a shot at him, thinking he was one of the killers come back to finish the job.

LEX FOUND a shovel in one of the sheds, and tossed it up into the coach seat, then climbed up, set his Winchester in the boot beside him, and grabbed the reins. A hundred yards behind the ruins of the station house, a small creek, lined with brush and a handful of scraggly cottonwoods, wound off toward the southeast. Clucking to the team, he jerked the reins and got the coach in motion. He'd never driven so clumsy a vehicle, but he didn't have far to go, and it was easier than dragging the bodies down on horseback.

At the creekbank, he looped the reins over the brake handle, then climbed to the running board, reached in for the shovel, and dropped it on the ground, before snatching the Winchester and jumping off. Moving into the brush, he found some soft earth—easier digging than the stony ground around the station—and used the edge of the shovel to mark off three rough rectangles.

The thick grass made for tough going until he peeled the turf back, then the shovel cut easily into the damp ground. It took nearly two hours to excavate the shallow graves, and he was drenched with sweat for the better part of the digging.

When he'd squared off the graves, he stabbed the shovel into the mound of dirt and walked to the creek to get a drink. Kneeling beside the swift, shallow stream, he bent over, immersed his head, and mopped his neck with a neckerchief, then slaked his thirst. He felt the water trickle down under his collar and across his chest and shoulders. It felt odd, almost as if a woman were tracing some invisible lines on his skin with the tip of a fingernail.

Somewhat refreshed, he walked back to the coach and opened the door. Reaching inside, he took the first corpse by the shoulders and hauled the man out, letting the legs dangle for a moment until he backed away, when the dead man's bootheels struck the ground with dull thuds.

Lex carried the body to the nearest of the three graves, lay the body on the ground, then knelt to check for identification. But the dead man's pockets were empty. Whatever papers he had been carrying were probably still in his wallet, wherever the hell that might be. Lex lowered the body into the shallow hole, then went back for the second man. Like the first, the second body had empty pockets.

Lowering it into the grave, Lex took a deep breath. The last victim would be the worst. He picked up the shovel and his Winchester and walked slowly back to the ruined way station. Hesitating at the chimney, he bent over to check the heat of the ashes. They were still warm, but only a single tendril of almost white smoke curled away from the ruins. Stepping gingerly, he moved toward the center of the burnt-out station, now little more than a mound of charred wood, and stopped by the ribcage he'd uncovered earlier.

Somewhere, he knew, the rest of the body lay under the ashes, and he used the shovel to pry loose a slab of charred wood. It felt as if it weighed almost nothing as he pushed it aside. The skull lay there, its jaw gaping, its eye sockets full of cinders. Using the shovel, he scraped away some more ash until the entire skeleton lay bare. It looked so fragile. Some of the bones had cracked from the heat, and all were blackened except the ribcage and skull, which were a dull gray.

Lex remembered a piece of canvas he'd seen in one of the sheds, and sprinted over to get it. Rushing back to the edge of the ruins, he spread it flat, and then used the shovel to scoop the bones out of the ashes. Removing the last of the bones, all small, the fingers and toes, he let them slide onto the mounded skeleton and shook his head, then knelt by the edge of the canvas. Rolling it closed, he bent both ends in, then scooted to the other side and rolled that edge in until he had a tight cylinder, like a rolled carpet.

He laid the rifle and shovel on top, then bent and slid his hands under the canvas roll and tried its weight. It wasn't very heavy, and he straightened up, cradling the remains in his arms, and walked toward the creek again.

Lex deposited the skeleton, still rolled in the canvas, in the last grave, and started to shovel dirt on top of all three bodies. It took nearly an hour to cover them all. After patting the last of the soil into three rough mounds, he tossed the shovel to one side, then took off his hat to bow his head.

He wasn't much for praying, but he did his best, his voice sounding hollow to his ears, almost as if it were echoing. Then, without a backward glance, he snatched the shovel and Winchester up, climbed into the coach, and brought it back to the outbuildings. Unhitching the team, Lex drove the four horses into the corral and made sure they had food and water.

He gave the desolate station one more quick look and, when he saw nothing he hadn't already seen, walked to the chestnut and swung into the saddle. It was almost sundown, but there was no point in staying where he was, and he nudged the chestnut into a trot, picking up the stage road and heading toward El Paso. He wouldn't ride all the way that night, but wanted to get some distance between himself and the ruined station.

As he rode, he tried to understand what had happened. Some folks, he knew, would assume Indians had been responsible, but he knew better. There was no sign of Indians, either Comanches or Apaches, and it was unlikely either tribe had raided the station. He knew that Victorio was still on the loose, and that the Comanches still left the reservation from time to time, but this attack had the feel of white men.

He knew without having to confront the question directly that Wade Daltrey had had something to do with it. But without witnesses, it would be difficult to prove. The murders would just be three more bits of the legend that Daltrey had accumulated around him, sometimes getting credit for things he hadn't done, and sometimes slaughtering his victims so anonymously that no one ever made the connection.

Maybe Walter Perkins would have some answers,

but it seemed unlikely. Perkins was forty or fifty miles away, and probably had no idea the station had even been attacked. But Lex was troubled. The two men in the coach were almost certainly passengers. But there had been no sign of the coach driver, and he probably had a shotgun rider as well. That assumed that the body in the ashes belonged to the station master. But if it didn't, then he, too, was missing.

It was nearly ten o'clock by the time Lex stopped for the night. He found a small stream and pitched his camp under some willows. He wasn't hungry, but wanted a fire, and gathered some dead wood from along the creek bank. He got it going with some dry grass and twigs, then fed a few of the larger pieces of wood into the flames.

He unsaddled and watered the chestnut, then tethered him in a patch of grass. Using his saddle for a pillow, he rolled into his blanket and watched the flames, trying to fit together the day's events with what he had already known about Wade Daltrey. The attack had been senseless, but that wouldn't have mattered to the one-time major.

Closing his eyes, he drifted off, hoping that the morning would make more sense to him than the current day had, but knowing it wouldn't.

Something woke him, and he sat upright, his eyes trying to adjust to the gloom. Overhead, the stars were smears of cold light that blurred as he glanced at the sky, then resolved as his vision slowly adapted. The chestnut nickered nervously, and he knew that was what had awakened him.

Lex reached for his Colt and eased it out of the holster. Holding his breath, he listened to the night.

Except for the clop of the chestnut's hooves as it shifted nervously on its tether, it was still. Then he heard the chirp of a cricket in the grass to his left, and the response of a second, further away.

A frog croaked, a deep booming sound, then splashed into the creek. More frogs joined in, as if they had been spooked by something and now felt their courage returning. Lex stood up, setting the blanket aside carefully, trying to avoid the rustle of cloth as he got to his feet.

For a moment he thought about calling out, but reconsidered when he realized that if someone were trying to sneak up on him, it would be better to let that person think he'd not been detected.

Moving toward the chestnut in a crouch, he kept his eyes on the open country to the east. Once past the horse, he got down on one knee, then lay flat, trying to use the starlight to pick out a silhouette. It was a long shot. Anyone trying to surprise him would probably crawl to minimize the chance of discovery. So far, there was no sign.

Then the frogs went quiet again. The cricket stopped chirping, and all he could hear was the breathing of the chestnut. Crawling toward the horse, he stayed on his knees as he reached up to pull the Winchester from its boot. He backed away from the chestnut, still on his knees, and slid the safety off, trying to muffle the sound with his palm.

Lex held his breath, listening for the least sound: the hiss of cloth on grass, the click of a dislodged pebble, even the thud of a carelessly placed foot. Nothing.

But he was convinced someone was out there.

Then he heard a thump, the sound of a body hitting the ground followed by the rush of air driven from lungs. Muffled curses then, the sound of anger turned inward as someone cursed himself for his stupidity. There was a groan then, and a sharp intake of breath.

Lex saw him then, a man on his knees, trying to get to his feet. Another groan, and the man pitched forward onto his face. Lex wasn't sure, but it appeared that the man had made no attempt to break his fall, as if he were unconscious or too tired to care.

Lex crept through the grass until he reached the stony ground away from the creek. The man hadn't moved, and hadn't made another sound, but Lex wasn't about to take chances. He kept creeping forward until he could just make out the outline of the man's body on the ground, a shapeless mound of shadow.

Lex watched him for more than a minute. A slight movement caused by the barely audible breathing told him the man was alive, but whether he was conscious or not, Lex couldn't tell.

He moved forward again until he was able to reach out and touch the prostrate form. As his fingers closed over the cloth of the man's shirt just below the shoulder, Lex saw the man start for a second, but he made no move to turn or to look at Lex.

Then Lex realized his fingers were sticky. He shook the man a little harder. "Mister," he hissed, "you all right?"

The man groaned, but made no other answer. Lex laid the Winchester on the ground and reached for the man with both hands. Another groan as Lex started to pull the man by his shoulders.

Lex got to his knees and rolled the man over onto his back. In the darkness, it was all but impossible to see what he looked like or how badly he had been injured, but Lex was unwilling to strike a match. If the man had been shot, then it was possible that he was being pursued, perhaps closely. It was just too risky to give away his position.

Getting to his feet, Lex reached down to take the man by his shoulders, and started to drag him back toward the camp. The wounded man was not small, and it was no easy matter to haul him through the darkness, but finally Lex felt grass under his heels, and he knew he was getting close.

He nearly tripped over his bedroll, all but invisible in the gloom, and laid the man down on his blanket. Lex moved back into the open to retrieve the Winchester, then dashed back to the stranger, and knelt beside him. He'd have to see what he could do to stop the bleeding in the dark.

Ripping the sleeve from the man's shirt, he let his fingers grope along the thickly muscled arm until he found a hole in the biceps. Tracing around the back, he found where the bullet had passed through, and wrapped the sleeve tightly around the arm, then knotted it. He didn't like the idea of not cleaning the wound, but that would have to wait until morning.

Quickly Lex patted the man down, looking for some other sign of injury and, when he found none, breathed a sigh of relief. The man had obviously lost a lot of blood, but he would survive. Lex covered him with his blanket, then found a tree and sat back to wait for daylight.

As an afterthought, he went back to take the man's sidearm from its holster and tucked it into his belt before retaking his seat. There was no question of any more sleep that night.

AS THE sky started to turn gray, Lex gathered more wood for the fire, tiptoeing around the sleeping man. Once he got the fire going and put up a pot of coffee, he scrutinized his mysterious guest. The man appeared to be in his late forties, a little on the heavy side, with a beard that was auburn, shading toward gray at the temples. His skin was darkened by the sun, and leathery, as if he'd been the outdoor type. His breathing was shallow but regular, and it seemed he was going to make it all right.

Lex wondered whether the man might be the driver of the stage coach, but the answer to that question would have to wait until the man woke up. He threw some beans and bacon in a frying pan, and watched while the beans turned to gooey paste as the bacon curled and spat as it bubbled in the bottom of the pan.

He ate quietly, careful not even to scrape the tin plate with his fork. When he was finished, he went to the creek and washed the plate and fork. Then he sipped his black coffee quietly, waiting for the man to wake up.

At sun-up, his impatience getting the better of him, he knelt by the sleeping man's side and shook him by the shoulder. The man groaned, then swiped a hand toward Lex the way a man tries to chase a fly in his sleep. After a second and a third shake, the man opened his eyes.

"Who the hell are you?" he demanded, trying to sit up. The effort contorted his upper body and he grabbed at his shoulder. "Jaysus Christ, that hurts!"

"What happened to you?" Lex asked.

The man blinked his eyes, tried again to sit up, and this time managed. He reached for his holster, felt the empty space where the butt of his pistol should have been, then screwed up his face as he peered at Lex. Reaching into his shirt pocket, he pulled out a pair of wire-rimmed spectacles, hooked the temples over his ears, and blinked once more. Finally, he answered Lex's question. "Who wants to know?"

"Lex Cranshaw . . ." The Ranger stuck out a hand which hung in the air for a long moment while the man examined it as if he thought it might somehow pose a threat to him. When it was apparent that the hand was what it seemed to be, he took it reluctantly in his own.

"Timothy O'Leary," he said. But he volunteered nothing more.

"Who shot you?" Lex asked.

"How you expect me to know that? There was a dozen of 'em, maybe more. I was too busy running to take names."

Lex nodded. If it would take dental pliers to get the information he wanted, he would pull teeth.

"This happen at the stage station?"

"Aye, it did." O'Leary leaned forward a bit to scrutinize Lex more closely. "How did you know that?"

"I figured," Lex said, shrugging. Two could play dentist. He waited for O'Leary to volunteer more information, and when he didn't, Lex asked, "You the driver?"

O'Leary nodded. "I was, yeah."

"How many passengers did you have?"

"Two."

"Shotgun rider?"

O'Leary snorted. "That'll be the day. Sure and if the day ever comes when Matt Harrison is willing to pay two men for the same trip, I've died and gone to greener pastures." He reached into his pocket again, this time pulling out a tobacco pouch and matches. He rolled a cigarette, offered the fixings to Lex, who declined, then tucked the pouch away before striking a match and lighting up. Wreathed in smoke, he asked, "You a lawman or something?"

Lex nodded. "Texas Ranger."

"I figured. What, with all them questions you was askin', it had to be that or some nosy newspaper man. But you don't look much like a scrivener, so . . ." he shrugged. Patting his shoulder, he nodded at the makeshift bandage. "You patched me up, I guess?"

When Lex said nothing, O'Leary nodded again. "Thank you," he said. He took a deep breath, seeming to relax a bit. "I reckon I shouldn't be so prickly. Didn't mean nothing, but it was a hellacious day."

"I understand. You want to tell me about it?"

"Not much to tell. We was on time. I make sure of that. Always have. Kind of a point of pride, I guess.

Me mother used to insist on that, God rest her, and it stayed with me. Anyhow"—he paused to take a drag on the cigarette, then expelled a thin stream of smoke—"like I said, we was on time. I got down from the coach and went to a tool shed. Wanted to tighten the brakes. A bolt was comin' loose and, anyhow, I was on the way back when all hell broke loose."

"Indians?"

O'Leary snorted. "I wish. No, it was white men, although they was worse than any Indians I ever seen. They had Al Latham, that's the station master, at gunpoint, and they was hauling the passengers out of the coach. One of the passengers, I don't know which 'cause I couldn't see and they was still inside, must have gone for his gun, or put up some sort of a fight, cause they started shooting every which way. Shot Al like a dog, they did, then blazed away at the coach."

"For no reason?"

O'Leary grunted. "You gonna shoot an unarmed man in the back, do you need a reason?" When Lex shook his head, the driver pushed on. "Anyhow, I started to run, and they seen me. Bullets was flyin' all over the place. One of 'em winged me, but I kept on runnin'. No way I was gonna take on that many men. Not with just a Colt. My shotgun was still up in the coach seat. Even with that old Remington, I don't know that I would have tried anything. Al was already dead, and them passengers was pincushions for sure. They was banging away at the coach from both sides. It's a wonder they didn't kill one another, now I think of it."

"You know who they were?"

O'Leary shook his head wearily. "Mr. Cranshaw, I don't travel in them circles. Never seen 'em before, but there's one, I swear, I'll recognize him if I see him again. Big fella, must be over six feet, black beard. He was the boss of the outfit, that much I'm sure of. I heard about him, and I think I know his name, but . . ."

"Anything else you can remember?"

O'Leary shook his head. "Nope."

"Latham alone at the station?"

"Since Patricia, Mrs. Latham she was, died last year."

"And you don't remember anything else about them?"

"They was raggedy. Looked like some sort of uniform on the big one with the beard, but I ain't sure."

"What sort of uniform?"

O'Leary shrugged. "Had a hat with braid on it. Gold braid. And pants with a stripe. Could have been faded brown, rust, something like that."

"Butternut?"

"Rebs, you mean? Hell, I don't know. Could be. But, like I said, that was just the big one. The others was like any pack of cowboys, far as their clothes."

"You carrying any freight? A payroll, anything like that?"

"Nope."

"Do you normally?"

O'Leary shook his head. "Not for more than a year now, since Mr. Harrison tried to up his price and lost the contract for the Army payroll. Used to carry a strongbox once a month, headed for Arizona Territory.

But that's been over a long time. Why you askin'?"

"Just trying to figure out why they attacked the coach, is all," Lex said.

"Let me tell you something, Mr. Cranshaw. I been held up more than once. This wasn't about money. Leastways, not only that. This was plain meanness. They could have had what they wanted and ever'body could have walked away healthy. They killed them men because they enjoyed it. And that's a fact!"

Lex rubbed his chin. "How's the arm?"

O'Leary smiled. "Still there. I been winged before and I reckon I been hurt worse."

"You came all this way on foot?"

The driver nodded. "There wasn't no time to saddle up, Cranshaw. Like I said, bullets was flyin' ever'where. I guess I'm lucky I got out alive."

"You can believe that," Lex said. "I buried three men. Your two passengers and one other."

"Chubby lad? Ginger hair and mustache?"

Lex shook his head. "I don't know."

"What do you mean, you don't know? You throw people in the ground, you ought to see whether they're breathing, at least. You must know what he looked like . . ."

Lex shook his head again. "They burned the way station. The body was inside. Just bones left. I'm sorry."

O'Leary's lip trembled then. "Jaysus!" Shaking his head, he crossed himself. "They didn't have to do that," he muttered. "It ain't right!"

"Latham was a friend of yours?"

"Only one I got. Known him for years. Used to go

fishing whenever we could spare the time. Him and Patty was like family. When she died, well . . ." He choked back a sob, and looked away. Lex left him to himself, and went to the fire to pour coffee. He came back with a cup and offered the scalding liquid to O'Leary, who shook his head.

"Not hungry," he said. Then, looking up at Lex, he said, "You know who done it, don't you?"

Lex nodded.

"Who. You tell me who it was, dammit!"

"No need, Mr. O'Leary. I'll take care of it."

"The hell you will! Tell me the bastard's name!"

"Wade Daltrey."

"Him!"

Lex nodded. "That's why I'm here."

"Heard about him. But I never seen him. I just didn't figure . . . hell, I thought it was just stories."

"It's not fiction, Mr. O'Leary. Drink your coffee. I'll make you some grub." He thrust the cup at O'Leary again, making to let go so the driver had no choice but to grab the handle. Getting the plate again, he poured a little water in, added beans and a couple of strips of bacon, and set the plate in the fire.

"We'll have to ride double," he said, squatting over the fire to tend the food. "El Paso's a long walk. And we have to get that arm tended to."

"Patterson place ain't far. I know Dan. I can get a mount there."

"I have to see the U.S. marshal in El Paso. He's . . ."

"Walt Perkins?" O'Leary snorted. "What for?"

"He sent a letter to Austin. That's what brought me out here. Seems Daltrey's been riding roughshod over a quarter of the state. But he made the mistake of stealing some horses from the governor's cousin."

"Ain't that just like . . . you know, you can rob from the little man all you want, but God help you if you mess with a politician or his kin. But I'll tell you one thing, Perkins ain't gonna help you none."

"Why do you say that?"

"'Cause I know him. He's worthless. Scared of his own shadow. How in hell he got a badge, I don't know. Less'n he got a cousin, too."

"Still, I ought to check in with him."

O'Leary nodded. "You want help, you got it."

Cranshaw looked at him sideways.

"Don't you look at me like that, Cranshaw. Daltrey's got to pay for what he done to Al Latham. I want to be there when he does."

DAN PATTERSON'S ranch was ten miles from the campsite, and it took Lex nearly three hours to reach it. Carrying double, the chestnut was laboring, and Lex stopped frequently. At one point, he even walked for a couple of miles, letting the horse walk at its own pace while O'Leary slumbered in the saddle. Still weak from loss of blood, the stage driver was game, but asking a lot of himself.

Lex knew O'Leary wanted to go with him to El Paso, and knew it was probably not a good idea. But he had to find an irrefutable argument, one that would shut O'Leary up immediately, and keep him shut up long enough for Lex to make his getaway. He was hoping that the driver would stay at Patterson's to recuperate, leaving him free to push on to El Paso by himself. Rather than risk O'Leary's wrath, he chose to keep the plan to himself, thinking that Patterson would agree and, together, they could convince the older man that he was too weak to travel.

The country ahead was rugged: long, sloping valleys full of tough grass, sliced by deep ravines like the jagged scars left by a dull knife, and studded with buttes, layer on layer of colored stone that seemed to ripple in the sunlight, as if each stratum changed color with the one below it, then the next and the one after that. It was a product of the shimmering heat, but the effect was starkly beautiful.

When they were getting close to the Patterson spread, O'Leary seemed to come awake, almost as if he sensed something. Lex was walking again at the moment, and asked the driver how he was feeling.

"Arm's kinda stiffened up on me," O'Leary told him. "Other than that, I'm fit as a fiddle."

"How fit's that, Mr. O'Leary? I've heard some awful sick fiddles in my time. Never did care for the sound of one."

O'Leary grinned at him, wrinkling his leathery face and showing his thick, tobacco-stained teeth. "That's for sure then you never heard me play a jig, laddie. I get me hands on a violin, I'll show you a thing or two. Maybe Dan's got one I can borry."

"Don't go to any trouble on my account, Mr. O'Leary."

"No trouble, son. Be a pleasure. For both of us."

They were working their way up a long slope, and Lex was beginning to feel the heat. O'Leary noticed. "Maybe you and me should change places," he suggested. "I can walk a ways."

"Not such a good idea. Because I'm bushed, and if you get tuckered out, we'll both be in trouble. I'll just walk until we get to the top of this rise, then we'll take a rest. Downhill, I think the horse can carry us both, unless it's too steep."

Saving breath and energy, Lex lapsed into silence.

When they reached the hilltop, O'Leary reined in, and straightened in the saddle. Lex stood alongside the chestnut, staring out at the broad, sweeping valley spread out before him. Dozens of horses, maybe two hundred in all, grazed on the valley bottom, casually switching their tails as they moved along both sides of a broad, slow-moving stream studded with small islands full of brush and scrub oak and, here and there, a willow.

The sun made the water look as if it were silvered over, almost bleaching the reflection of blue sky and willow completely away. Ripples as the current swept past submerged sandbars sent blinding swords of sunlight in every direction. Several thin-legged birds waded in the shallows at one end of the largest island.

"That's Dan Patterson's land," O'Leary said, in a voice that couldn't conceal the pride.

"You seem to know him pretty well," Lex said.

O'Leary nodded, then grew somber. "Used to be my son-in-law."

"Used to be?"

"I lost my daughter three years ago. I ain't got over it yet. Neither has Dan. Sheila was . . . never mind."

"I'm sorry, Mr. O'Leary."

Forcing a laugh, the driver said, "Don't be. The grim reaper'll get us all, one day. But not before I introduce him to Wade Daltrey."

O'Leary slipped from the saddle, groaning as he lowered himself to the ground. Lex helped him sit, then dropped to the ground beside him. The driver pulled out his tobacco. "Want me to roll you one?" he asked.

Lex shook his head. "No thanks. I just want to catch my breath and give my legs a break."

He watched the horses for a minute or so, then noticed that they were starting to react to something. Most of them had stopped grazing and raised their heads, either to sniff the air for some scent, or because they'd heard something, Lex wasn't sure which.

A moment later, something caught his eye off to right, at the far end of the valley. A small dust cloud ballooned on the far side of the stream, just beyond a stand of cottonwoods. He could make out the figures of two or three men on horseback. They were riding flat out, as if chasing someone, but there was no sign of anyone, mounted or on foot, ahead of them. Then it dawned on Lex. They were *being* chased.

Getting to his feet, he dug his binoculars from his saddlebags, and slipped them from their worn leather case. Training them on the men, now several hundred yards away from the willows, he could see them more clearly. Two of them were looking over their shoulders, and as Lex swept the glasses in that direction, he saw why. Six or eight more men were lashing their own mounts with their reins, trying to close the gap.

He thought immediately of Daltrey, and checked the pursuers one by one, but none of the men wore the kind of hat O'Leary had described. If they were Daltrey's men, he wasn't with them.

The first burst of gunfire confused him, even though he'd seen the white puffs mushroom around the chests of the second band of riders. At that distance, the sound was almost toylike, a barely audible crackle, more like someone stepping on brittle leaves at a great distance than explosions propelling lethal projectiles. But then, he thought, after Shiloh, it would take a great deal of gunfire indeed to make an impression.

The three men in the lead were still far ahead. One of them returned fire, but he wasn't trying to hit anything, just keep the pursuit honest. Lex watched, wondering whether he should mount up and join in. But he had no idea what the squabble, if that's what it was, was all about. His horse was beat, and he was almost exhausted himself. Taking sides without knowing anything was bad enough, but in the shape he and the chestnut were in, he would be lucky if he didn't get himself killed.

The fleeing riders were slowly pulling away, and it seemed to Lex that the pursuers were slowly slacking off, as if they had made their point, whatever it might be, and were content to let their quarry escape. The three riders veered away and started uphill on the far side of the stream, angling up the gentle slope almost as if they meant to circle back around, but when they reached the top of the slope, they broke on over the far side and disappeared.

"You figure out what's happening?" O'Leary said, suddenly reminding Lex that he wasn't alone.

Shaking his head, Lex shifted his gaze back to the larger group of men, who were now slowing up, just as they reached a small group of horses grazing at the water's edge. "Nope. But it's getting interesting. Looks to me like those men down there are about to take some of your friend's horses. Here, see if you know any of them." He handed the binoculars to O'Leary.

The driver adjusted the focus and leaned forward, as if the extra foot he gained might make a difference. He shook his head. "Nope! Never seen any of 'em, far as I can tell. Then, I don't know all Danny's men."

Another distant crack drifted across the valley and up the slope, and Lex jerked his head around, trying to pinpoint the spot. He thought he saw a cloud of gunsmoke far up the opposite slope, somewhere just below the crest, but couldn't be sure in the bright sunlight.

Looking back at the men by the creek bank, he saw a spout of water geyser up ten yards out into the stream, and now he knew someone was firing at the men below.

Training the glasses on the hilltop, Lex saw that the three men he'd first seen had doubled back. They were now in a position to rain fire down on the men at the creekbank. The odds were against them, but they had the advantage of position.

The eight men at the waterline seemed to stop for a moment, as if one of them were shouting orders. Suddenly, like an amoeba dividing, the amorphous group split in half. Four men headed on toward the small herd and the other four dismounted, grabbing rifles as they tugged their horses into some brush along the creek.

The men were no longer visible, but Lex could plot their location by the small clouds of gunsmoke wafting up and out of the bushes. The men on the knoll had settled down to a steady fire. So far, they hadn't split up themselves. All three stayed on the hilltop, content now to pin the others down.

Turning to the four who'd approached the herd, Lex could see that they had now cut nearly two dozen mounts from the larger group and were pushing them back along the creek. While he watched, they drove the horses into the water and crossed through a gap in the brush up onto the near bank.

For a moment, Lex thought horses and men were going to charge straight up the slope toward him, but a hundred yards from the water, they turned off, heading now parallel to the creek, well out of rifle range from the opposite hilltop.

In the meantime, the four men in the brush had started to work their way up the far hill, leapfrogging one another, firing as much to keep their opponents' heads down as for real effect. The lead man was almost halfway up the hill, heading straight toward the rifleman in the middle.

Whatever else these men were, they weren't cowards. It took more than a little courage to charge uphill under the muzzles of men intent on killing you if they could.

The first man on the hilltop wavered, starting to get to his feet, then dropping out of sight as he started to crawl along the crest toward the others. A moment later, all three got to their feet and ran. The men on the slope fired a ragged volley, but no one was hit, and the men on the ridge top darted to their left and down out of sight.

It occurred to Lex that they might be going for their horses, hoping to charge over the ridge line before the men on the slope below were able to get back to their own mounts. The men on the hillside must have been thinking the same thing, because they held their ground.

The horses were almost to the end of the valley now, heading toward a vee-shaped gap in a steep hill that closed off the western end. Two of the drivers turned back, galloping toward the creek and on across. They ran flat out, parallel to the water, and sat at the bottom, below where the riflemen still waited on the slope.

They fired one shot each to get the attention of their comrades and, when one of them turned, the mounted men waved their hands, signaling the men to come down. They would provide cover in case the three men on the ridge reappeared. But as time dragged on, it seemed less and less likely.

When the four men had raced down the slope and into the brush, they mounted their horses, their hats suddenly bobbing into view over the upper branches of the scrub. As soon as they were in the open, the two guards turned their own mounts, and all six men raced across the creek.

Lex glanced toward the end of the valley, but the horses were already out of sight. The six men in the valley bottom were racing hard to catch up.

"If that don't beat all," O'Leary mumbled, reminding Lex once more that he had company. "Damndest thing I ever seen. I'd love to know what the hell that was all about."

"Only two things it could be, Mr. O'Leary," Lex said.

"And what might those be?"

"Either somebody just stole two dozen prime horses from your friend Dan Patterson, or somebody just stopped those same horses from being rustled before it could get fairly started. And either way, I'd bet a month's pay we just saw some of Wade Daltrey's handiwork."

WALTER PERKINS was sitting behind his desk, his feet propped up on one corner, and his arms folded behind his back. Squat and pasty-faced, he reminded Lex of a turnip, with blue buttons for eyes. A thin mustache, like a piece of string, traced the line of his upper lip and curled downward at either end, as if gravity were too much for the sparse hair to withstand.

His head was bobbing, and Lex waited until it stopped before saying, "What do you know about Wade Daltrey?"

Perkins smiled. "Everything there is to know, I guess. You going to bring him in?"

Lex nodded. "That's why I'm here."

"Good luck."

"You sent to Austin, didn't you?"

"That's right, I did. Needed help. But I don't figure you're gonna be much. I figure we need a whole passel of men armed to the teeth. I tried to get the Army interested, but they don't seem to care very much. Look's like ole Wade is gonna be around a while yet."

"Why's that?"

"Because you don't have a chance in hell of bringing him in. He's got too many men, and he moves too quick. Been on the run for years, and I don't reckon one man will make a whole lot of difference in that regard."

"I thought you'd help," Lex said, lowering himself into a rickety ladder-back chair.

"Think again, Cranshaw. No way am I going after that bloodthirsty rattler with one man."

"What about the people around here? Can't you deputize a few of them?"

"Easier to make wine outta well water. These folks are scared snotless, and they don't mind tellin' you so."

"What about you?"

"I'm forty-two years old, Cranshaw. I didn't live this long by sticking my head in a grizzly's mouth. Not in my line of work. You want Daltrey in a hurry, you best plan on doing it your own self. I'll wait until I get some real help, thank you."

Lex nodded. "You know where he is now?"

"Nope."

"No idea?"

"None."

"You know he burned a stage station about fifty miles from here a couple of days ago, don't you?"

"If you say so."

"And that he ran off almost two dozen horses from Dan Patterson's spread yesterday?"

"That a fact?"

Lex sighed in exasperation. "If I understand you correctly, you're telling me that you wrote to the cap-

ital for help, and now you don't plan to do anything.
Is that about right?"

"I guess."

Lex stood up. "Thanks for nothing."

"Look, Cranshaw. I appreciate that you come a
long way. I want to see Wade Daltrey swing from a
rope, just like everybody else around here. God
knows, he deserves it, but . . ."

"But you want somebody else to put the noose
around his neck. You want somebody else to kick the
chair out from under him. And as far as you're concerned, he can hang there till he rots, as long as you
don't have to lift a finger. Did I leave anything out?"

"Just one thing . . ."

"What's that?"

"Where you want your effects sent?"

Lex turned and left, trying to swallow his anger,
and knowing that if Perkins was that frightened of
Wade Daltrey, everybody else in the area was twice
as scared. Dan Patterson had hinted as much, without coming out and saying so. Taking a deep breath,
Lex shrugged his shoulders. If that's the way it has to
be, he thought, that's the way it's gonna be.

But where to start? Daltrey was close, that much
was certain. He seemed to be heading west, at least
if the attack on the stage and the theft of Patterson's
horses meant anything. In geometry, it took two
points to determine a line, but there was no reason
to believe that Daltrey was moving in a straight line.
He could have headed anywhere after getting the
fresh mounts. In fact, the number of horses stolen
suggested that Daltrey was planning to do a lot of
hard riding.

He could be planning on going to New Mexico or Arizona, maybe even California. Or he could head north, up into Missouri, where Quantrill had wreaked such havoc for so long. The fact was, and Lex couldn't avoid it, he needed Daltrey's men to raid again before he could know where to begin.

Something told him he was going to be out a long while, and he might as well stock up on supplies. He walked to his horse and the spare mount Patterson had given him, and unhitched the reins. Walking down the street, he found the general store and tied up in front.

Inside, it was cool and smelled of metal and oil, spices and seed. Behind the counter, a thick-waisted man in an apron stretched over his belly taut as a sausage skin smiled at him. "What can I do for you?" he asked.

"Need some beans and bacon, some cornmeal, and some coffee."

"How much?"

"Enough for two weeks, at least."

The man looked at him with his head cocked to one side, as if he were appraising a piece of horse-flesh. "Don't look like a big eater to me, so I guess I can put a bundle together for you." He started to gather the items on the shopping list. "Where you headed?" he asked.

"Not sure." Lex said. "Just know I'm gonna be on the trail a while."

The storekeeper nodded. "You want to be careful once you get away from town, mister."

"Why's that?"

"Not safe. Feller named Daltrey is tearing hell out

of the country from here to hell and back. He's a bad one. What I hear is he's heading south, but that's probably just a rumor. If you're headed that way, though, I'd be real careful."

Lex pricked up his ears. "South, you say?"

"Yup. Couple of his boys was in the saloon last night. The way I hear it, they was talking about lifting Injun scalps for bounty. Seems like some Mexicans is paying fifty dollars a scalp for Apache hair."

"You sure about that?"

The shopkeeper grew suddenly suspicious. He stopped what he was doing and wrapped his hands in the apron as he turned to face Lex. "You seem awful interested. He a friend of yours or something?"

Lex shook his head. "Never met the man, but I plan to."

The merchant screwed up his eyes, shook his head, then turned back to gathering Lex's order. "Whatever you say. But you best be careful." Hefting a bag of flour and dropping it to tamp down the contents, he rolled the top closed and said, "Anything else?"

Lex nodded. "A couple of boxes of shells. Forty-fives."

"You got it." The storekeeper moved along behind the counter, tapping boxes with one thick finger until he found what he was looking for. He grabbed the boxes of cartridges and slid them along the counter until they bumped into the sacks. "That it?"

"For now, yup."

With a thick-leaded pencil, he scratched the prices in a column, licked the pencil, and totaled the order. "Be eleven fourteen. We can round 'er off at eleven.

How's that?" he looked up from his calculations.

Lex reached into his pocket for the money, unfolded some bills and peeled off the correct amount. He pushed the bills across the counter and watched as the merchant packed the supplies into a larger package.

"You be careful out there, mister. Daltrey ain't too likely to want somebody he don't know come sniffin' around. I was you, I'd forget all about lookin' for him."

Lex smiled. "Can't forget about it," he said. "It's my job."

The shopkeeper looked surprised. "You the law? I didn't see no badge, so naturally I . . . Anyhow, sorry I was so suspicious. I didn't mean nothing."

"Forget it. Anything else you can remember?"

The merchant shook his head. "Not really. Them boys was pretty drunk, so I hear, and they wasn't talking much. Once they got themselves a couple of gals, they pretty much had only one thing on their minds."

Lex searched a corner of his mouth with the tip of his tongue. He wondered whether or not to ask the next question, but this might be his best lead, and he couldn't afford to pass on it. "Where can I find these girls?"

"Over to the *del Norte Saloon*. One of 'em was named Jess. I don't know what the other gal's name is. Wasn't there, and the missus don't take kindly to me even knowing about such women, if you know what I mean."

Picking up his parcel, Lex said, "Thanks." He touched the brim of his hat and left the store. After packing his supplies into the spare saddlebags

Patterson had lent him, he looked for the saloon. It was a block away, and looked to be doing a good business despite the early hour.

Lex went inside and took a table. Three or four girls in flashy dresses, cut low and accented with more frills than a millinery window, were waiting on tables, flirting with the motley assortment of early drinkers, and bantering with the bartender.

One of them spotted Lex at his table and sauntered over. "What can I get you, mister?" she asked.

"A beer'll be fine."

"Buy me one?"

"Actually, I'm looking for a woman."

"What do you think I am," she said, leaning forward and running one long nail down the bridge of his nose. "Maybe you been on the trail so long you forgot?"

Lex grinned. "I meant a particular woman."

"I'm nothing, if not particular, honey," she said. "What'd you have in mind?"

"I'm looking for someone named Jess."

"Jess what?"

"Don't know."

She straightened up then. "Why's it you're looking for her?"

"Want to ask her some questions."

"What sort of questions?"

"Sorry, but that's between me and Jess."

"I'll be right back," she said, twirling away and heading toward the bar. She waited while the bartender drew a draft, then came back with the beer, set it down on the table and said, "I'm Jess. What do you want?"

"Any place we can talk privately?"

"In this town? You must be joking." She looked suddenly coy. "Unless you want to come to my room. I can keep a secret pretty good, and nobody else knows what goes on there."

"All right." Lex took a sip of the beer.

"It'll cost you."

"How much?"

"How much you got?" She stuck the tip of her tongue between her lips, then gave him a smile that made her look ten years younger. "Only teasing you," she said. "Come on."

Lex followed her upstairs.

JESS HADN'T known much, or if she had, she hadn't been willing to spill it. She did say that the man she was with the night before said he was camped with some friends about twenty miles to the southwest, on Eagle Creek. She said she didn't know how many "friends" were with him, or whether one of them was Wade Daltrey.

It was the best lead he had, and Lex decided he had no choice but to follow it. As he rode southwest, the terrain got more and more arid, and less hospitable. Ravines and buttes were more prevalent, and what flatlands there were tended to be rocky and hedged in by steep walls. There wasn't much water, and what little there was was sluggish and salty.

Lex was making good time. The chestnut was fresh after an overnight rest, and the horse Dan Patterson had given him was lively and more than equal to keeping up. Once more the sun hammered down, and by noon he felt as if he were wrapped in a thick blanket soaked in hot water. Everything ahead was blurred, partly by the intense heat radiating off the barren ground and partly by the perspiration that kept seeping into his eyes.

As he rode, Lex kept wishing he had Al Hensley along. The sergeant was a good man in a fight, and they had been through more than their share of tough times together. But Hensley was somewhere in East Texas, and no amount of wishing would change that. He wondered what he would do if he found the men he was looking for and if their leader was Wade Daltrey. But he knew that was putting a rather large cart before a relatively unsteady foal. First, he had to find them. What came next he would worry about when the time came.

Lex was no stranger to long odds. Shiloh had, by far, been the longest, and he hoped to God, or whatever indifferent spirit passed for one, that he'd never have to go through something like that again. But his career as a Ranger had brought him close more often than he cared to remember. He'd done battle with the worst in the worst of men, and seen the best in the best of them. But the nature of his work brought him into far more frequent contact with the former than with the latter. And if the information he had was even halfway accurate, it would happen again in a matter of hours.

He was ready, but there was always a little voice in the back of his mind at a time like this, whispering "What happens if . . ." The if was never explained, but there was no need. He knew how the blank was filled in. And it was easy to tell himself that he was more than able to take care of himself, in this world or the next, should it come that.

But that was facile, almost outright self-deception, and he knew it. No one really wanted to die. But some people lived their lives as if they didn't care one way or the other. Wade Daltrey, apparently, was one of them. And in Lex's experience, men like that were usually more than happy to bring a few extra passengers along into the afterlife—the more the merrier, in fact.

By two o'clock, he had looked at the situation from every conceivable angle twice over. And it was no less bleak than it had been at the start. What he knew was sketchy, but it seemed that he was pursuing no fewer than nine men, possibly more, who had all the fresh horses they needed, and a decided thirst for blood. They presumably were well armed and, since law enforcement was, by its very nature, reactive, they had the initiative.

By three, he was close to the headwaters of Eagle Creek. The stream rose out of a small lake, fed by a spring, and drifted southwest toward the Rio Grande at the Texas–New Mexico border. Daltrey was taking a chance, whether he knew it or not, because the Apaches were getting restive. Some had already bolted off the reservation and some had never been there at all. The mountains of New Mexico had been home to thousands of them, including one of their most prominent chiefs, Victorio. If Daltrey meant to take on Apaches, hostile or otherwise, he might be biting off more than he could chew.

At best, they would skin him and stake him out, bathed in honey, on an anthill. At worst, he would start an uprising that would take dozens of innocent lives. Even if the Apaches got Daltrey, once aroused, they would be like hornets. There was no telling where, or if, they would stop. And Lex knew that he was himself taking a desperate chance heading into Apache territory.

If there were hostiles in the area, or if Daltrey managed to provoke peaceable Indians, Lex would look no different to them. One white man on an anthill was as good as another. That was the Apache philosophy and, were he in their shoes, Lex had to allow that he would probably look at things the same way. It may not be logical, but it sure as hell was consistent. And once somebody lied to you, you weren't too likely to give the benefit of the doubt to the next man.

His reverie was so deep that he nearly missed the sound of gunfire in the distance. Something alerted him, and he reined in, confused but aware that something had happened. Then he heard it clearly. It was heavy fire, but distant.

Lashing the chestnut, he headed through a narrow draw a hundred yards ahead, not certain where the firing was coming from. The terrain was mazelike, alternately winding ravines and jagged buttes, causing any sound to echo in a hundred directions. He wasn't sure whether he was listening to continuing volleys or more sporadic fire reverberating through the countless channels that crisscrossed the country in every direction.

By the time he was halfway through the draw, it sounded like the shooting was somewhere behind him. He was forced to rein in once more and strain his ears to try to pinpoint the source. Shaking his head in frustration, he spurred the chestnut and kicked it on through the draw, the gunfire now drowned out by the sound of his horses' hooves.

At the far end of the ravine, he stopped a third time. There was a thick silence, as if the previous turmoil had been a figment of his imagination. He was about to move on when a short volley exploded, still very distant, sounding as much like halfhearted applause in a nearly empty theater as like gunfire.

There was only one way to be sure, and he slid from the saddle, tied the chestnut to a twisted chaparral, and started to climb up the nearest high point. It was a steep rock face, the layers of sediment broken unevenly, and allowing him uncertain hand and footholds as he crabbed his way up. He had to test each outcropping to make sure it was secure, and twice he pulled hunks of rock free, in the process showering his head and shoulders with sand and slivers of brittle stone.

As he scrambled higher, he found himself in the paradoxical position of hoping the gunfire continued, whatever its cause, until he could locate its origin. Some small trees studded the rock face, their trunks perpendicular to their spidery grasp of the stone. Reaching for one, he felt the rock under his left foot give way, and grasped desperately for the slender trunk, hoping the roots were securely anchored.

The sapling began to bend as he swung his leg hip-high looking for another foothold, found one with the toe of his boot, and dug in. At the same moment, he heard the shriek of roots tearing free and dug his hand into the clotted soil and lacy roots of another. Something skittered across his hand, and he glanced over in time to see a scorpion, its tail coiled high over its back, about to sting him. He snapped his wrist, tossing the insect away in a low arc, and grabbed on again.

He felt as if his lungs were about to burn through

his ribcage, and he clung there motionless for a minute or more, listening to the distant sound of rifles and the internal barrage as his heart pounded against his chest. Knowing that time was running out, he started up the wall again, and as he neared the top, he suddenly could hear the gunfire more clearly.

Looking back over his shoulder, he realized he had climbed above the rim of the opposite wall. The sun was to his left, meaning he was facing north. That put the source of the gunfire somewhere to the south or southwest, if his ears were to be trusted. He climbed the last fifteen feet with reckless stretches and only cursory attention to the security of his holds. As he hauled himself up over the rim, a chunk of the ledge under his right hand broke loose, and he narrowly avoided breaking a leg as the huge slab of stone glanced off the wall just beyond his right foot on its way down.

Standing there on the rim, he heaved a sigh, took several deep breaths, and shielded his eyes as he looked for any tell-tale signs off to the south and west. The brilliant glare seemed to be even harsher across the draw, and he unslung his binoculars to bring them up to his eyes.

He detected a faint haze, possibly gunsmoke, but it was so vague he couldn't be sure. The gunfire continued, though, and he was sure now it was coming from the southwest, possibly from the same place he thought he saw the haze. It was difficult to judge distance through the blazing sun, but he guessed he had three or four miles to go, and that was assuming the route was no more tortuous than it had been so far.

He marked the spot by reference to the sun,

knowing that once he dropped below the rimrock, it would be his only guide. He would be winding in and out of these ravines, detouring left and right, and, if luck weren't with him, probably taking more than one blind alley, hurrying to the scene of action that would be long finished well before he arrived. But it was the only thing he could do. There was a good chance, better than even in fact, that Wade Daltrey was behind one of the guns. This might be his best and even his only chance to find Daltrey and his men in this barren wilderness, and he could not afford to pass it up.

He descended recklessly, conscious of the fading sound of the gunfire, and hurrying as if he feared it would stop altogether before he reached the bottom of the draw. He dropped the last ten feet after looking over his shoulder to make sure the ground was even and safe. Scrambling to his feet, he untethered the horses and leapt into the saddle.

Using the sun, he zigzagged through the interlacing ravines, sometimes doubling back on himself as he followed the beds of long-dead rivers, some barely wide enough to permit two horses to pass abreast. On the sandy ground, he could see the traces of past flash floods from cloudbursts.

An hour later he no longer heard the guns, and he wondered whether he had managed to close the gap at all. He was working his way through a broad, shallow canyon now, following the bed of a shallow creek. It was two hundred yards wide, in some places even more, and unlike most of the deep gouges in the earth, this one supported lush grass.

Far ahead, the canyon curved gently to the left,

and the creek bent with it, its broad, smooth surface reflecting the sunlight so brilliantly it looked like a flaming Saracen sword. The going was relatively easy now, and the canyon seemed to drift generally in the direction he wanted to go. He'd already traveled five or six miles, but had no sense of how far he was from his original vantage point in crow miles.

As he swept through the curve, he thought he could smell gunsmoke, and when he broke into a broad valley, he saw a gray pall hanging in the air. But it wasn't just gunsmoke. Far ahead, nearly two miles through the next valley, he saw three or four columns of smoke. As he drew closer, the tang of burning skin and hair was unmistakable, and he tried to imagine what could be burning. But his mind's eye recoiled from the single vision that kept pushing its way to the front of his consciousness: the charred bones at the way station.

As if drawn to that horrible thought by some gigantic magnet, he pushed the horses even harder. He could see the bases of the columns of smoke now, and knew what was burning: wickiups. An Apache *ranchería*, a little more than a mile away now, had been set ablaze. The hide coverings of the wickiups accounted for the tang in the air.

He slowed now, realizing that if there were Apaches still in the *ranchería*, he would be seen as an enemy. Knowing that he was being overly cautious, knowing that if there *were* Apaches still in the area, they already knew he was here, he dismounted, tugged the horses into some brush to tether them, and grabbed his Winchester.

Lex broke into a run, darting from one clump of

thick brush to the next, zigzagging over the open ground and keeping his eyes on the wickiups. There was no sign of life—no horses, no barking dogs, nothing. He picked up his pace, trying to push from his mind the thought that whatever had happened here, he was too late to do anything about it.

He nearly stumbled over the first body, all but hidden by thick brush, just one leg jutting out into the open. He knew immediately that it had to be a child. The leg was so thin, the legginged foot so tiny. He knelt and reached into the brush to push it aside. He saw the face then, but couldn't tell whether it was a boy or girl.

The scalp was gone.

LEX KNEW now that the Apaches had abandoned the *ranchería*, if any of them had survived. But there was no way to tell who had attacked the small camp. Only six wickiups had been built, and four of them were burnt-out shells. The other two were charred over a large area as if they had been doused with something flammable which had burned off before the hides had burst into flame.

He watched from the brush for several minutes just to be sure, but he hadn't heard a sound. It was possible, he knew, that a military unit had found the camp and attacked it, but the scalping of the child made that less likely than it might have been. The most brutal assaults on the Apache, as on most other Indians, Lex knew, had been perpetrated by white "volunteers" or "irregulars." These were men more interested in killing than in justice. Lex knew that he was probably in the minority in holding that opinion, but he didn't give a damn. He knew what he knew, and wasn't about to pretend otherwise.

Once he was convinced that the *ranchería* was deserted, he started to creep forward, keeping his ears open for any sound that might herald the return of the warriors. It was possible that the camp had been undefended, more often than not the situation that obtained when assaults were launched. The volunteers always found it easier to kill women and children than full-grown warriors. If that were the case, the men might return at any moment. And they would not bother to ask whose side he was on.

It was also possible that the warriors had fought off the assault, then pursued the attackers, whoever they might be, leaving the dead for burial on their return. If that were the case, though, he would have expected a token force, a handful of people, perhaps just women or old men, to tend to the wounded. But so far there were no wounded. None.

With every step he took toward the center of the half-circle, open to the east, he felt the muscles in his neck and shoulders grow a little more taut. It was almost as if he were turning a ratchet, increasing the tension by his own movement.

The air was full of repellent smells. The burned hides and singed hair from the wickiups was the strongest, but almost hidden in that overwhelming stench was the tang of gunsmoke and, under that, all but obscured, the sickeningly sweet fragrance of fresh blood. He was certain the child would not be the only victim. He only hoped there weren't too many more.

As he reached the last clump of brush, the last effective cover between him and the ruined wickiups, he called out in Spanish. "Hola!"

He got no answer, but hadn't really expected one. "Amigos?"

Still no answer.

Holding his breath, as if even the faint whisper or an exhalation might change everything, he twisted his head to try to relieve the tension. He felt the muscles in his neck and shoulders pop, then took a deep breath and stepped into the open. To indicate his peaceful intentions, he lowered the Winchester. It was pointless, anyway, to carry it ready for firing, because if an Apache warrior were watching him, he'd be dead long before his finger twitched in the trigger guard.

He saw the second body then. Once more, just the legs were visible, this time jutting through the open entrance to one of the intact wickiups. He lay his rifle down and rushed to the lodge, entered partway, and knelt beside the still figure. This time it was an old man. Like the child, he had been scalped.

Lex closed his eyes for a moment. When he opened them, they had started to become accustomed to the gloom of the wickiup's interior. Without seeing clearly, he knew there was another victim in the lodge. Reaching for a match, he struck it with a thumbnail, and held it over his head. The feeble flame didn't cast much light, but it was enough for him to see that his suspicions were correct.

Before he could see any details, the match burned all the way down, searing his fingers even as he shook it out and let it fall. He backed out of the lodge and got to his feet. The village campfire was almost out, but two or three brands about the thickness of his wrist still burned in the center of the circle of rocks. He walked to the fire, grabbed the longest of the brands and snatched it from the flames.

Walking slowly back to the wickiup, he shifted the

brand in his hand, changed hands for a moment to wipe his sweaty palm on his jeans, then took the brand back into his right hand and knelt before the entrance. Easing past the body of the old man, he raised the makeshift torch aloft. Two more bodies, another old man and a woman, obviously pregnant, lay against the wall. He didn't have to look closely to see that they, too, had been scalped.

The lodges smelled of death, a thickness that hung in the air, moist and foul. Shaking his head in disgust and rage, he left the wickiup and moved to the next. It was empty. He searched the ruins of the four lodges that had been torched. Finding two more bodies, neither one of them a warrior or young woman, he tried to understand what had happened in the small village.

Where were the young men? Where were the young women? They would not have run off, not if they were able to fight, and, knowing what he did about Apaches, even if they weren't. They would have died in their *ranchería* rather than leave their families defenseless. But there was nothing in the ruins to tell him what had happened, nothing in the way of evidence to tell him whether it had been a military raid or other Indians or Wade Daltrey.

He doubted it had been a war party, even of Comanches or Kiowa strayed off the reservation. But that, too, would have accounted for the scalping. Lex moved beyond the wickiups into the brush along the creek. Working his way in a zigzag pattern back and forth through the clumps of scrub oak amd sagebrush, chaparral and ocotillo, he tried to find some evidence that would explain the carnage.

But he found nothing.

What he needed was some indication which way the raiders, whoever they might have been, had gone. Until he found some reason to change his mind, he was going to operate in the belief that Wade Daltrey and his men had been behind the attack. The bare patches of ground showed an occasional boot or moccasin print, but there were no signs of horses, shod or unshod, anywhere in the scrub.

Changing his tack, he made a circuit of the small *rancheria*, then another and a third. He found one more body nearly a hundred yards from the back of the semi-circle, but still no evidence of a large body of mounted men. If it had been an army assault, there would have been some sign. They would not have left their horses.

Comanches might have. So would Kiowa, but then there would have been more moccasin prints. Moving along the creek bank, he found several footprints clustered together in the damp earth just above the waterline. Looking back at the *rancheria*, he thought the ground unnaturally smooth, then, dropping to one knee, he looked more closely at the soil. It was relatively dry, but the coating of dusty sand showed a lacy network of fine lines. He knew then what had happened.

Someone, presumably the attackers, had used branches to wipe out as many tracks as they could. But they hadn't been able to hide the impressions in the damp sand at the waterline. Looking more closely at the creekbed, he saw dozens of shallow depressions. Already, they were almost full of silt deposited by the sluggish current. Had the water been any swifter, the prints would already have been erased.

By the orientation of heel and toe on the white men's boots, he knew they headed upstream. Lex sprinted back to his horses, tugged them out of the brush, and swung into the saddle. He nudged the chestnut toward the creek, the spare horse tugging at the tie line as if reluctant to follow. Entering the creek, Lex scanned the bank on either side. He had no idea which way the raiders had gone, but they had to leave the safety of the streambed sooner or later. The further from the camp they traveled before doing so, the less careful they would be.

Working his way slowly upstream, he checked each bank for several yards, then pushed on. Every twenty or thirty yards, he'd rein in and scan the next stretch of the stream. He was getting impatient, and hated to be moving so slowly, but there was nothing to be done. If he missed the place where the raiders had come out, he could ride for miles before realizing it, then have to ride back just as slowly as he now moved. As it was, the raiders already had three hours or so on their head start. And with every pause he made, their lead lengthened.

He'd gone more than two miles before he found what he was looking for. As he'd suspected, no attempt had been made to disguise the exit, as if the raiders felt that they had outwitted any pursuit. Either that, or they were so confident, they felt they didn't have to worry who followed. But then why bother to use the creek at all?

And judging by the numbers, they had little reason to worry. There were so many hoofprints, he couldn't be sure how many horses there were. But as near as he could tell, there were at least two dozen, and probably more. The strange thing was the number of moccasin prints. There appeared to be at least a dozen different sets, and most had been made later than the hoofprints, because it was easy to see where they had partially obliterated hoofprints. The edges of the moccasin outlines often cut right through the unmistakable arc of an iron shoe. Some of the prints were cookie-cutter perfect. And there was no mistaking the fact that they had been made almost simultaneously.

As he sat there in the saddle, the chestnut's front leg on the bank, the back still in the water, he tried to understand the significance of what he was seeing. Could the raiders have been Indians after all? There was no doubt the prints had been made by Apache moccasins. The distinctive upturned toe was clear as day. But most of the prints were on the small side, suggesting either women or children, perhaps both. It was almost certain that warriors would not have brought along their families if they were tracking the raiders who had destroyed their *ranchería* and killed their family members.

Putting the puzzle aside, Lex urged the chestnut on up the creek bank and started ahead, glad of a chance to ride at something approximating a reasonable pace.

It was starting to get late, and he glanced at the sun just before following the tracks into a narrow ravine. Its walls were forty or fifty feet high in most places, and it was no more than thirty or forty yards across at its widest. Some distance ahead, Lex could see where it narrowed even further. Already one half was full of shadow where the sun could no longer reach. He had less than an hour until sundown, and knew he was not going to catch his quarry before then. But that wasn't his only problem. There was the chance that the raiders might stop early and if he weren't careful, he might end up riding right up their backs, before he even knew they were there.

If they were at all cautious, they probably had a rear guard, somebody to keep an eye on their backs, just in case there was some pursuit. As he entered the ravine, he saw something that puzzled him. There was a swath, maybe three feet wide, that wiped out all traces for several yards. It was far too late and too pointless for it to have been an attempt at concealing the tracks.

He reined in, draped his forearms over the saddle horn and studied the ground. Chewing on his lower lip, he decided to dismount, and looped the reins over the pommel before slipping from the saddle. Kneeling at the front end of the strange swath, he saw that moccasin prints resumed, as well as the presence of a pair of oval depressions.

Lex had no idea what had made them or whether they were significant. He looked back the way he'd come for a moment, then got to his feet. Shaking his head in bafflement, he looked back at the ground in front of him and noticed a second pair of depressions. He could have smacked himself—it was so damned obvious, now. The depressions had been made by knees, small knees, the knees of someone who had fallen and been dragged for several yards, wiping out all traces of whomever had gone ahead.

The moccasins were not those of a war party in pursuit. They were the prints of prisoners. That would explain the small size. Women and children.

But what would Daltrey want with prisoners?

That was one question that would have to wait for an answer. Just one. Among many.

LEX PUSHED on until it grew too dark to see the trail. He pitched a camp against the base of a canyon wall. Reluctant to risk a fire, he contented himself with rolling into his blanket and huddling against the chill. He felt guilty about not burying the dead at the *ranchería,* but there were so many bodies, and there was so little time. And he didn't know enough about Apache custom to risk inadvertently doing something that would affect the dead's place in the afterlife.

He had no idea where the raiders were, but couldn't shake the feeling that he was getting close. Despite their head start, they had to have been hampered by their prisoners. What Lex couldn't understand was why they took prisoners at all. The shopkeeper in El Paso had told him Daltrey was planning to collect the bounty on Apaches' scalps. Jess, the girl at the saloon, had told him the same thing. Why take the trouble of dragging along prisoners? At best, they would slow Daltrey down. At worst, they posed a threat that could not be overlooked. Apache women were fighters every bit as fierce as the men.

And if they were fighting for the very lives of their children, there was no limit to the amount of hardship they would be willing to endure, and no risk they wouldn't take.

It made no sense, unless it wasn't Daltrey at all. An army unit would take prisoners, perhaps to force a wayward band of hostiles back onto the reservation at Warm Springs or White Mountain. But the trail was leading into Mexico, and unless in hot pursuit, the American military was forbidden to cross the border.

Could it be a Mexican army unit, Lex wondered. But that didn't make sense, either. The Mexicans were justly infamous for their brutal treatment of the Apache. They wouldn't bother to take prisoners. If they had an advantage that enabled them to make the capture, they would have slaughtered their prisoners on the spot and run like hell. And they were notorious for avoiding combat with Apaches at all cost, unless their superiority in numbers was so great that victory was guaranteed. Numbers that large would have left a more evident trail, and would have left Apache bodies strewn around the *ranchería* camp rather than dragging them along.

No matter how he looked at it, Lex was forced to the conclusion that he was following Wade Daltrey. He tried to sleep, but the tangled web kept ensnaring him and he would follow another strand until he got hopelessly lost. The canyon was full of shadows, and there was no moon, just the hard, glittering light of the stars far overhead. He watched the constellations, trying to lull himself to sleep, but it didn't help.

All around him, small trees were masses of gray, whispering in a cool breeze. Sitting up, he tossed the blanket aside and walked to the creek for a drink of water. As he knelt at the water's edge, he heard something downstream, something that sounded like a branch breaking underfoot. He straightened up, still on his knees, to listen. A rustle of leaves, faint but definite, drifted toward him, just audible over the gurgling of the current.

Lex ran back to his campsite and grabbed his Winchester. He moved close to the wall and started downstream, toward the sound. For several minutes, he heard nothing but his own breathing and the crunch of sand and gravel under his own feet.

Then there was a rush of footsteps. Someone shouted. More footsteps, this time heavier, and he heard someone panting, running hard, shoving branches aside and kicking small stones in the darkness. Whoever it was didn't worry about being heard. Lex moved away from the wall toward the creek, from where the sounds seemed to emanate.

Another shout, in English. Someone splashed into the creek then. He could hear rapid footsteps, then a second splash as another runner plunged into the shallow creek. Lex reached the stream a moment later. The noise was coming from a few hundred yards downstream, and he moved parallel to the streambed, trying to keep low as he sprinted in a crouch.

The splashing sound stopped, and he heard a woman's voice, speaking a language that was neither

English nor Spanish. It was guttural and hissed, but hard to hear. It had to be Apache, Lex thought. An Apache woman. The woman screamed then, and there was a third sudden loud splash. Lex could make out almost nothing in the poor light downstream. But he was closing rapidly.

Not knowing who he would find, he couldn't just rush into the open. As near as he could tell, there were just two people. Worming his way through the brush, less concerned about noise now as the splashing continued, he shoved branches aside with the extended rifle.

Slowly, two figures emerged out of the gloom, right at the water's edge. Both were standing in the creek. The water was no more than a foot or eighteen inches deep at that point, and the taller of the two figures seemed to be getting the better of the struggle.

As Lex stepped out of the brush, he was no more than fifty yards away. With the dark growth massed behind him, he knew he would be hard to see, and he bent low and charged toward the water. He could see them now, a tall man in a checkered shirt and jeans was wrestling with a much smaller woman. As Lex neared the water, still twenty yards upstream, he heard the shriek of tearing cloth and the woman fell backward. The cowboy cursed under his breath and dove at the woman, who was backpedaling, her legs still in the water, her stiff arms on the slippery bank.

She lost her purchase and fell into the creek as the big man landed in the water right beside her.

The man swung his fist, and Lex heard the impact

of knuckle on bone. The woman sank deeper into the water and the man struggled to his feet and grabbed her by the hair. He heard Lex coming then, but it was too late. He looked upstream, leaning into the darkness as Lex barreled into him, shoulder first, and knocked him backward into the creek.

Before he could regain his footing, the big man found the muzzle of the Ranger's Winchester pressed against his forehead.

"Not a word," Lex hissed.

"The hell are you?" the man said, then gave a yelp as Lex shoved the rifle a little harder.

"You ain't gonna . . ."

Lex swung the Winchester around and slammed the stock into the big man's temple. The cowboy fell back with a surprisingly quiet splash, and lay there unconscious, the water lapping at his head and shoulders. Lex bent to grab him by the heels and tugged him out of the creek, dropped him unceremoniously in the sand, and turned to the woman.

She was unconscious, her head resting against the creekbank. Lex bent over her, and saw an ugly gash along her left cheek, deep enough that the bone was exposed. He didn't know what she'd been hit with, but it had really done a job.

Her dress had been ripped down the front, and several scratches on her chest oozed blood that looked almost black in the dim light. Lex pulled her out of the creek and put her down the grass. As he knelt beside her, she moaned. Her head rolled from side to side, then her eyes opened. Even in the darkness, Lex could see the terror. He held a finger to her lips, but she was too frightened to obey. Trying to sit up, she opened her mouth to scream again, and Lex clamped a hand over her mouth.

She clawed at the back of his hand for several seconds, Lex shaking his head, trying to reassure her. The clawing stopped, and Lex slowly relaxed the pressure. In Spanish, he whispered, "Are you all right?"

Her head bobbed, and Lex took his hand away completely. "I'm going to get some rope," he said. Jerking his head toward the unconscious cowboy, he added. "We have to tie him up. How many more are there?"

"¿Qué?"

"How many men?"

She shook her had. "No men," she said. "Just women and children."

"No, I mean, how many men were there who attacked your *ranchería*?"

She nodded then. "Eleven, twelve," she told him, shrugging to indicate it was just a guess.

Lex took a deep breath. He knew the odds were long, but this was worse than he had imagined.

"And how many prisoners?"

"Thirteen. Eight women and five children."

"I have to go back to my camp," he said again, "to get some rope to tie him up." He stood up and extended a hand. "Come with me." She grasped the offered hand, and he pulled her to her feet. But when he started to move away, she shook her head.

"I'll stay here," she said. "I'll watch him."

"You're not afraid?"

As if to demonstrate how little fear the unconscious man instilled in her, she walked over to him and spat into his face, then kicked him in the ribs. "I'm not afraid," she said.

"All right. But if you hear anyone coming to look for him, hide yourself."

She nodded that she understood. Lex sprinted along the bank of the creek, less concerned about noise than speed. He knew what the cowboy had had in mind for the woman. What he didn't know was whether the man had intended to be just the first, or the only one to have his way. But regardless of which it was, sooner or later, the man would be missed. Even an outfit like Daltrey's would have enough discipline to realize that one of its men had been gone longer than he should have been.

Whether they would come looking immediately or wait till morning, Lex couldn't guess, and couldn't really afford to. He had to assume that they would come almost as soon as they realized he was missing.

When he reached his camp, Lex snatched at a lariat without slowing down, turned in a tight circle and raced back downstream. He slowed as he drew near the site of the attack, then stopped altogether to listen.

He heard a heavy thud, then a second and a third, just as he was about to resume his sprint. He found the scene of the struggle at the edge of the creek, and turned in, where he had dragged the unconscious man.

He could see virtually nothing in the thick gloom, and leaned ahead, almost tempted to grope his way along with an extended hand for guidance. Calling out softly for the woman, he waited for her answer, but heard nothing. Once more, he whispered to her.

Perfect silence swallowed the sound of his voice. He could see the channels gouged by the unconscious man's heels in the dirt, so he knew he had the right place. Why didn't the woman answer? Had the cowboy come to sooner than expected and overpowered her? Automatically, he levered a round into the chamber of the Winchester. The deadly click might give him away, but it would also make anyone lying in ambush think twice about jumping him. That was an edge he couldn't pass up.

When there was no sound from the Apache woman, he moved ahead several more yards, then saw the man's boots, toes up, sticking toward him from a clump of brush. He didn't remember having taken the man that far from the stream.

Something was wrong.

Holding his breath and listening, he heard nothing but the babble of the creek and the chirp of insects in the weeds. Moving into the brush a few yards away from the feet, he slid in behind, just in case any one lay in wait, prepared to jump him as soon as he bent down to tie the man's legs.

But there was no one hiding there. The woman seemed to have vanished. Moving into the open again, he grabbed the man's feet and tugged him into the clear. And he knew why the woman had disappeared.

The man's face was gone. Where his nose and beard should have been, there was nothing but a bloody pulp. The skull had been crushed, and in the darkness, Lex could just make out clots of brain tissue extruded through the shattered sutures of the bone.

The woman had had her own revenge.

And now she was gone.

LEX SPRINTED back to his camp. He had hoped to interrogate the prisoner, learn whatever he could about Daltrey's plans. But the Apache woman had closed that door before he even got his hand on the knob. He had to figure that Daltrey's men would come looking for the dead man, if not immediately, then first thing in the morning. He couldn't afford to let them know he was there. Breaking camp in a hurry, he thanked his stars he hadn't bothered with a fire. Packing up, he mounted the chestnut and headed back through the canyon. In the darkness, in alien terrain, he had to move more slowly than he would have liked, but there was nothing to be done about it.

And now, with the Apache woman loose, he knew she would try to find the warriors from her *ranchería*. There was even a chance that they were nearby, if they had come back to the carnage and picked up the trail. Apaches were notorious for their tracking ability. They could follow the faintest trail in the dead of night, and had been known to travel a hundred miles on foot in less than twenty-four hours. Once the warriors returned to their village and found what had happened, they would be out for revenge. The last thing Lex needed was to get caught in the middle, assuming the Apaches were willing to concede there *was* a middle.

Lex headed into the creek and moved upstream. The horses would muddy the water, but there was a good chance that the darkness would screen the disturbance, at least for a few hours. He crossed his fingers and hoped Daltrey's men were too tired to come looking before daybreak.

Two miles upstream, a fork of Eagle Creek veered in from the northeast while the main course came in from due north. If he took the branch, he might be able to circle back and position himself to the southeast. Once Eagle Creek flowed into the flatlands approaching the Rio Grande, he'd be able to pick up the trail again rather easily.

When he reached the fork, Lex took the smaller stream without hesitating. The ground sloped gently uphill, and in less than a mile, he was able to leave the creekbed and head back to the south over a barren tableland. There was very little cover, but as long as he stayed away from the creek in its shallow valley, there would be no risk of being seen until daylight.

He was exhausted, and had to get some shut-eye. At three o'clock, he reined in, hopeful that he had doubled back enough to confuse any pursuit. And he knew that any search for the dead man might be short-circuited once they found his body. Not knowing what had happened, Daltrey's men might get skittish. If they thought Apache warriors were on their trail, they just might run for the river.

He left his horse saddled, tethered it to some sage,

the follow horse beside it, and lay down to sleep, his Colt balanced on his chest. Over the years he'd been forced to learn to sleep lightly, and the ability had never been more welcome. Closing his eyes, he curled his fingers over the butt of the pistol, took a deep breath, and was off.

The first sunlight woke him. He came fully awake instantly, while the sky was still dark gray. The sun exploded in a burst of deep red and orange, then began to swell on the horizon, a bloody tick gorging itself on the edge of the world. He was in the saddle almost immediately, contenting himself with a swallow of water and some dried beef for breakfast. He chewed the stringy, salty meat as he rode.

By ten o'clock, he found himself approaching a steep escarpment overlooking a broad, shallow valley. Lex dismounted and crept to the edge, his binoculars still in their case around his neck. Just visible to the south, four or five miles away, was a sluggish expanse of the Rio Grande. Beyond it, the purple smear of the Sierra Madre mountains, a thin band of dark color separating the almost limitless beige expanse ahead from the pale blue sky above.

Using the glasses, he swept the flats from east to west, looking for some sign of Daltrey's band. Already gnawing at the back of his skull was the unpleasant probability that he would have to give up the chase or cross the border illegally. Lex Cranshaw was not a man who broke the law lightly. But neither was he a man who could forget the corpse of the small child at the *ranchería*, its skull bone laid bare by the scalper's knife. The very idea that someone was willing to pay money for a human being's flesh and

hair was appalling to him. That there were those willing to complete the transaction was unfathomable.

But Wade Daltrey was such a man, and he was
somewhere out there, another dozen innocent lives
in his hands for reasons Lex could only guess. If he
had to cross the river to stop Daltrey, there was little
doubt in his mind that he would do it. And if it meant
that he had to break the law, so be it.

But first he had to find Daltrey.

The flat, brush-studded plain ahead was silent and
motionless. Cactus was everywhere. Despite the
presence of the river a handful of miles away, the
arid flats were inhospitable to all but the hardiest of
plants. And the most desperate of men. Somewhere
to the west, Lex knew, Eagle Creek flowed into the
plain, crossed it, and emptied into the Rio Grande.

Getting to his feet, he walked slowly back to the
chestnut. The first order of business had to be to find
a way down onto the flatlands below. Mounting up,
he followed the ragged edge of the escarpment, looking for a trail. Sooner or later, he knew he'd come to
a switchback that worked its way down the hundred
feet or so. He hoped he happened on it before he
reached Eagle Creek.

It was nearly noon when he found it. Once more,
he dismounted to walk to the edge and search the
flats with his field glasses. There was still no sign of
Daltrey and Lex was starting to wonder whether he
had guessed wrong. Maybe Daltrey had turned back,
headed up into New Mexico, or dead west to
Arizona.

But there was nothing to be done about it now.
He had to be on the flats before he found Daltrey

and his men, otherwise the raiders would spot him as he came down off the bluff. Until he was able to get help, he had to keep the men in sight, not try to take them on single-handedly. That would be a fight he was bound to lose.

The trail down the face of the bluff was narrow and littered with shards of rock broken from the brittle layers of sediment that striped it. Rather than keep the follow-horse tied, he gave the roan some rope and held the lariat loosely in his hand. If one horse lost its footing and went down, the other would still have a chance.

The trail had five legs, descending twenty feet or so over a stretch of a hundred yards, then cutting back upon itself and dropping another twenty or thirty feet. It seemed like he held his breath the whole way down. He was hungry, and had to stop soon for food. When he entered the last leg, he looked up at the sheer rock face looming over him and felt a wave of dizziness wash over him. He closed his eyes, and wrapped his fingers around the lariat, fearful of losing his grip on it.

The dizziness passed, and the chestnut seemed to be relieved as it nearly galloped the last twenty yards to the flats. He could feel the strain in the tether to the follow horse.

Lex reined in, keeping close to the base of the bluff, and dismounted. He couldn't risk a fire, but gnawed ravenously at more dried meat. A cup of coffee would have seemed like heaven, but heaven would have to wait. He was bone tired, and the temptation to nap was almost irresistible. He knew he'd have an easier time fighting off his exhaustion if he were in the saddle, so he climbed back on the chestnut and started west. Keeping just far enough away from the steep wall to be safe from falling rocks, he followed the countours of the bluff.

The sun was ahead of him now, and he wondered where in hell Daltrey could be. The bluff was on his left, and had started to taper down toward him, a sure sign he was getting close to Eagle Creek. Suddenly he saw a rider materialize almost as if out of thin air. The man was nearly a mile ahead, and at that distance, his face was just a pale blur. The slanting rays of the sun didn't help. Lex reined in, dismounted, and tugged the two horses in behind a slab of rock canted against the face of the bluff.

Using the glasses again, he watched the man, who was standing in his stirrups and looking back over his shoulder as if impatient for someone to join him, trying to get a good look at his face. Another rider appeared, then several riderless horses. The first rider turned his mount and waved his arms furiously, trying to hurry someone.

More horses, then several more riders. Seven men, so far. Then Lex saw the first of the prisoners, a pair of women, yoked together, stumbling ahead. Their arms were tied behind their backs, and a rope had been looped around each of their necks, and one of the riders held the loose end in his hand. As Lex watched, the rider jerked the rope, and the second woman fell to her knees.

Five children came next, like the women, unmistakably Apache, at least in their dress. They were yoked together as well, then more women, five of them, a total of twelve captives in all. Several more horses darted into the open, tossing their manes and pawing the ground nervously, followed by more mounted men. Finally, the man Lex was waiting for: a big man, wearing remnants of Confederate butternut and a braided hat cockily riding his dark hair. His mouth opened and he yelled something Lex couldn't hear.

So that's Wade Daltrey, Lex thought. Horse thief, murderer, scalper of children. It'll be a rare pleasure to bring this animal in.

The stragglers caught up and coalesced into a ragged column. Daltrey moved to the head of the line and, with a wave that mocked the discipline of a cavalry commander, led the slow march toward the river. Lex watched for several minutes, debating whether to follow or turn back. But every time he told himself he ought not to cross the border, he could see the body of the dead Apache child sprawled in the dirt. Finally, he came, as he had known all along that he would, to the conclusion that there was no way on earth he was going to sit there and watch Wade Daltrey escape.

He waited until the tail of the column was almost invisible, then mounted up. The closer Daltrey came to the border, the less concerned he would be about pursuit. Even now, if worse came to worst, the raiders could leave their prisoners and sprint for the river, secure in the knowledge that lawful pursuit had to end at the water's edge.

But Lex Cranshaw was not interested in lawful pursuit. Not this time. Splitting legal hairs all too often let the guilty go free. Lex was interested in something else: justice. Wade Daltrey had to pay for his crimes, and no imaginary line was going to save him from the rope.

Lex kept the tail of the column in sight as it meandered toward the Rio Grande. Three miles behind, he wasn't worried for the moment about losing his quarry. Once across the river, he'd have to close up, because he had no idea where Daltrey was headed. The Apache woman had seen to that.

And on the Mexican side, he'd have another problem. The Mexican Army wasn't too likely to care about a few dead Indians, even if they were old men and women and children. It was, after all, the Governor of Chihuahua who had offered the bounty on Apache scalps. If forced to choose between a scalphunter with a fistful of Apache hair and a Ranger without permission, there was no doubt which way that decision would tilt.

The ground started to slope downward again, and the river was clearly visible in the distance. It looked more impressive now, broader and deeper. Lex had closed to within a mile and a half of the column, and sat on his horse watching, hands draped over the pommel of his saddle, as the first of the raiders nudged his mount down the shallow bank and out into the river.

One by one, the raiders entered the water. Two of them took charge of the herd of stolen horses, and three more drove the prisoners across as if they were some form of exotic livestock.

As they continued on into the barren wasteland of northern Chihuahua, Lex moved slowly toward the river. This was his last chance to change his mind. Once he crossed, he might as well see it through to completion, but as he edged along the bank, looking for a place to ford, he didn't hesitate.

He was halfway across before he looked back, wondering whether he was making the right choice. And if he'd ever make it back.

LEX FOLLOWED his quarry for two days. It seemed apparent that Daltrey knew where he was going, and that he was more than passingly familiar with the terrain. They had skirted several towns on their way, making wide loops to pass around the villages and the outlying farms, although there were few, and most were not very large.

The terrain grew more and more rugged as they drew closer to the mountains. The river valleys were fairly lush, but the vegetation ran along either shore and extended only a few hundred feet on either side before thinning out to saguaro, cactus, creosote, and ocotillo bushes. Most had thorns and few leaves worthy of the name. They were harsh and unforgiving plants, much like the land in which they grew.

Lex was beginning to wonder if there was any point in continuing the chase. Without help, he couldn't possibly take on Daltrey and his men. But there was no help to be had. Without authorization for the border crossing, he could not ask the Mexican authorities for assistance, and the people in the villages had no reason to worry about Daltrey as long as he passed on through. They had all they could do to eke a precarious living out of the arid wasteland they called home. Daltrey was irrelevant to them, unless he chose to pay attention to them. Then, and only then, they would fight.

On the morning of the third day, another small village loomed up ahead. Lex could see the spire of a Catholic church, its architecture like so many of the old missions he had seen in Arizona and New Mexico. But this time Daltrey was making straight for the village. Lex dismounted on the crest of a low hill and used the field glasses. He watched as the column straggled toward the village and went straight down the baked earth street toward the center of town, entered the central square, and dismounted.

Lex was a mile away, and knew he couldn't follow so close on Daltrey's heels without arousing the man's suspicion. But Lex had one advantage: Daltrey had no idea he was being followed. Lex waited until Daltrey and some of the others went into a cantina, leaving two men on guard with the captives, who huddled in a mass alongside the cantina like so many hunting dogs. Lex remounted and kicked his horse into a gallop, circling around to the south edge of the village and entering from the opposite end.

If one of Daltrey's men spotted him coming in, they would have no reason to believe Lex had been on their trail since the border. There was only the one cantina, and Lex was thirsty anyway, so he tied off in front of a ramshackle store whose peeling sign proclaimed it as a place of *general merchandise*.

He glanced at the Apaches as he walked past. The two guards glared at him but said nothing. He could feel their eyes on his back as he pushed inside the cantina. The sour smell hit him in the face like a pole-axe, but he ignored it, and walked to the bar.

He'd been in Mexico before, a long time ago. It was a period of his life he tried not to think about, but one that he couldn't ignore. He couldn't hear the Spanish language without thinking about Rosalita. He still missed her after all those years. He tried to push the thought away, knowing that it would just make him maudlin. He'd want to drink too much, knowing with every swallow that the whiskey wouldn't kill the pain, just numb it for a while. Then he'd feel bad in the morning and want to do it all over again. It was better to try to pretend that he'd never been married, that she had never died, taking their son with her, the two lives he most cared about cut down with one cruel slice of the reaper's scythe.

Cozying up to the bar, he waited for the chubby *cantinero* to take his order.

The man sported crazy patches of white hair from his chin and cheeks, not really a beard but anything but a close shave. "Is gringo day in Santa Mariá," he said, using English. "What you want to drink, señor?"

"Tequila."

"No bourbon, señor? I have good bourbon. This tequila, she will make your eyes bug out. Your throat will feel like you swallowed a piece of hell."

"That's all right."

"As you wish, señor." He grabbed one of several open bottles of tequila on a shelf behind him, where an old mirror, its silvering gray and scrofulous in patches, hung precariously at a slight angle. Wiping a cloudy glass with his shirt tail, he smiled at Lex, set the glass down, and slopped it full of tequila.

Lex paid for the drink, then walked to a table in the corner. He was able to see Daltrey at at table across the small room, three or four bottles and several glasses scattered on the table, and most of Daltrey's men crammed in around it. There was room, though, on either side of the boss.

The men were downing drinks almost as fast as they could pour them. Most were drinking tequila or mescal. Daltrey had what appeared to be his own bottle, a dark liquor, that he sipped without using a glass.

Lex tried not to stare, watching the *cantinero*, but keeping one eye on the former guerrilla chief. One of the men produced a deck of cards, and four men split off, taking their own table and one of the bottles. The conversation was raucous, and Lex listened for any clue that might tell him where Daltrey was headed.

The more they drank, the more rambunctious they became. The card game was punctuated with loud barks of laughter and the slap of cards on the wooden table top. The clinking of glass on glass filled the room. Clouds of thick smoke swirled over both tables as the men lit up small cigars and thick, hand-rolled cigarettes.

The card players killed their bottle, then tossed it across the room where it clattered against the base of the bar without breaking. One of the cowboys called for another bottle, and turned expectantly. The *cantinero* hadn't heard him or was determined to show a streak of stubborn independence, because he made no move to deliver the new bottle.

Instead of repeating his request, the cowboy got

up, knocking his chair over in his haste, and stormed up to the bar. "Where the hell's our bottle?" he demanded.

"Excuse me?" the *cantinero* said. "Señor?"

"Don't 'señor' me, asshole. We want another bottle. Where the hell is it?"

"Sorry, señor. I didn't hear you."

The cowboy jerked his pistol from its holster and seized the chubby man by his white mane. "Maybe you got something in your ear, amigo. Eh? That what it is?" He rammed the pistol into the *cantinero's* left ear and thumbed back the hammer. Twisting the gun back and forth, he made the barman cry out in pain.

Putting his gun away, he slammed the barman's head into the bar, then let go of his hair. "You got my order now?"

The *cantinero* swiped absently at a trickle of blood from his nose, then rubbed his forehead where it had smacked against the bar. "Señor," he said, "you didn't tell me what you want to drink."

"Don't give me that. I ought to . . ." He reached for his gun again and waved it under the barman's nose. It grew very quiet. Lex could hear the *cantinero* sniff, trying to stop the flow of blood. He pulled his own gun and thumbed back the hammer.

In the dead silence, everyone in the room heard the unmistakable click. "Maybe you should just tell the man what you want, then sit down," Lex said. "He'll bring it to you."

The cowboy spun around, the barrel of the Colt in his hand wavering uncertainly. He wasn't quite sure who had spoken and he leaned forward at the waist, trying to focus his whiskey-bleared eyes in the smoky gloom.

"Who asked you?" he said, his head still swiveling, trying to locate the man who had spoken.

"Nobody," Lex said. "I'm *telling* you."

Now the cowboy knew where he was. The muzzle of the Colt came around and held almost steady. The man teetered a bit on his feet, and had to keep adjusting his grip on the pistol. "Why don't you come on out of your rathole, there, and say that again?"

"What's the matter," Lex asked, "you don't understand plain English. Or are you too damn stupid?"

The man took a couple of steps toward the corner. Lex held his gun steady and stood up.

"Could shoot your damned eyes out at forty yards," the cowboy said.

"Not in the shape you're in, cowboy," Lex said.

"The hell I can't." He took another couple of steps, this time more cautiously, as if he weren't sure whether he wanted to go head to head with a man he didn't know.

He thumbed the hammer on his pistol back and smiled. "Want to see, asshole?"

Lex didn't wait. He leaped forward and to one side, bringing the barrel of his gun down over the drunken cowboy's wrist. The sharp crack of bone was clearly audible. The cowboy's gun dropped to the floor and he bent to retrieve it. It rattled as Lex kicked it away, then went off when it hit the wall. The report brought three of Daltrey's men to their feet.

The two guards burst in, their guns drawn, as Lex turned to the others. "He's all right," Lex said. "Just sober him up."

"Who the hell you think you are?" one of the guards snapped.

"A man who wants a little peace and quiet when he drinks," Lex said.

"Mind your own . . ."

"Man's right."

Lex knew it was Daltrey who had spoken. The voice was deep and rich, one used to giving orders that its owner knew would be obeyed.

"Get Eugene out of here," Daltrey snapped. "Take him outside and throw him in the goddamned horse trough. Do him good, prob'ly."

"But Wade, you ain't gonna let . . ."

"Now!" Daltrey said, this time his voice a hoarse whisper. "The rest of you sit the fuck down and play cards."

Daltrey got to his feet, snagged his bottle by its neck, and walked over to Lex. Without asking permission, he pulled up a chair and sat down. "You got sand, cowboy," he said. "I like that."

Lex sipped his tequila.

"What are you doing around these parts?" Daltrey asked.

"Passing through."

"Haw! Passing through, huh? Wish I had a dollar for every place I passed through in my life. What do you do for whiskey money?"

Lex shrugged. "Whatever comes along."

Daltrey looked at him appraisingly, his eyes hooded, his tongue jutting from the corner of his mouth. "I'll bet," he said finally. "You want a job?"

"Doing what?"

"See them Apaches outside, did you?"

Lex nodded.

"Them's mine. Like meat on the hoof, they are. I'm gonna sell 'em. There's some *Grande Ranchero* runs a bunch of mines. Uses slave labor, just like the good old days. You'd be surprised what he'll pay for strong backs. Then, of course, there's other ways to make money."

"That so?"

Daltrey nodded. "Interested?"

"No thanks."

Daltrey took a swig of the bottle. "I like the way you stood up to Eugene. Most men wouldn't do that, not in a room full of strangers. And especially when most of them strangers was friends of Eugene's."

"Some things just aren't right," Lex said.

Daltrey smiled. "Eugene don't know right from wrong. 'Course, he works for me. So maybe that's where he gets it, huh?"

"You'd know that better than I would."

Daltrey stuck his hand across the table suddenly. "Name's Wade. Wade Daltrey." He snapped the brim of his hat before adding, "Late of the Confederate Cavalry."

"Very late, I'd say," Lex observed. "War's been over a long time."

"For some folks, maybe. But some of us is soldiers through and through. It's in our blood. We *like* it, you see."

"Not for me, thanks, Wade," Lex said.

"You change your mind, I'll be around town for the rest of the day. Heading out in the morning, bright and early. Got to get them redskins sold while they still have market value." He stood up.

Lex downed his tequila as Daltrey walked back to his table. Lex got up. As he walked toward the door, Daltrey snapped him a salute. "See you around, cowboy," he hollered.

Damn right you will, Lex thought.

THE FOLLOWING morning, Daltrey was as good as his word. Lex watched from a hilltop south of Santa María as the column headed out once more. He'd been trying to decide whether Daltrey knew more than he let on the afternoon before. But no matter how he tried to rearrange the pieces, there was no way to make that possible. Had he suspected Lex of following him, it would have been too easy to eliminate Lex on the spot. Even assuming there was a lawman in the village, it was doubtful he'd be willing to risk his life to arrest Daltrey. The guerrilla commander had a clear shot. That he didn't take it could only mean that he had no reason to do so.

So Lex was at a loss as to why the man had offered him a job. He'd been straightforward in his offer, telling Lex what he was up to without hesitation. Whether it was the gringo superiority the Mexicans always commented on, or just plain indifference to the law or what Lex might think of him, Lex couldn't decide. Maybe both. Or maybe Wade Daltrey was so damned single-minded, he didn't see anything but his own ambitions.

The rolling hills were all but barren now, and Lex had to stay close to keep the column in sight. It was a fine line he was walking. Too close, and he ran the risk of being seen. Too far back, and he might lose Daltrey altogether. Even a party that size left little sign on the trail. The ground was baked to a ceramic glaze, there was no dust to kick up, even with all those horses, and the vegetation was so sparse it would be almost impossible to find broken grass or snapped twigs that meant anything even to a trained eye.

Or almost any trained eye, Lex thought. The Apaches were reputed to be able to follow a grasshopper through the desert, and even to tell how far ahead he might be. Lex didn't believe they were *that* good, but they were better than he was. And yet there had been no sign of anyone behind him; at least, none that he had been able to discover.

Shortly before noon, the ground started to slope dramatically upward. The column was sticking to the water courses now. Lex remembered a conversation he'd had with an old cavalry sergeant who'd seen his share of Indian warfare in the southwest. According to Brendan O'Murphy, who'd bought Lex a bottle of bourbon and then proceeded to drink all but the first shot he'd poured for Lex, that was the major difference between the white soldiers, or white-eyes, as the Apaches called the Army, and the Indians. The Indians always followed the high ground, balancing on the ridges like a roofer at the peak. It made them all but impossible to ambush. The military columns, on the other hand, stuck close to the water, partly for the sake of their horses and partly because the going was a hell of a lot easier.

"Cranshaw, me lad," O'Murphy had said, polishing off the last swig in the bottle, "the only time you see an Apache is when he wants you to know he's there. And that is God's honest truth. The gospel according to Saint Brendan." The old sergeant had fallen asleep after uttering his final bit of wisdom. Lex had never seen him again, but he had listened then with rapt attention, and now he found it all coming back to him, with even the lilt of O'Murphy's brogue intact. "They're the very divils, they are, lad. They'll rip out your heart and eat it raw for breakfast. But there's never been a soldier like them. Never. Give me a battalion o' the bastards and I can drive the limeys from Erin's fair soil all the way to the Indus River. That I can."

And the progress of the column seemed to sustain every judgment the old Irishman had made. While Daltrey's men seemed to wilt under the incessant heat, the prisoners seemed, if anything, to have developed a spring in their steps.

The column stopped more frequently now, and the rests grew longer and longer. The air was thinning and Lex was finding it harder to breathe, despite being on horseback. He'd already changed mounts once, shifting to the roan Patterson had given him to let the chestnut take a breather.

During one of the breaks, Lex sat on the ground, his back against a rock. He looked up at the sun between his fingers. The sky was white hot, the sun so powerful it was little more than the whitest spot against the blinding yellow-white glare. It looked as if the sky were on fire, or as if something had bleached its color away to nothing. His shirt was soaked through, and the rock behind him felt as if it had just been yanked from a blacksmith's hearth. His tongue was a strip of flypaper in his mouth. His lips were gluey, thick with a paste that collected at the corners of his mouth and dried to grains of sand.

He cradled his canteen in his lap, took a sparing sip of water to rinse away the glutinous mess, spat it into the dirt, then swallowed a mouthful. It felt good as it slid down his throat, despite its tepid temperature. He sipped again, capped the canteen, and hauled himself wearily to his feet.

They were somewhere in the foothills of the Sierra Madres, but the worst of the mountains were still far ahead. Lex hoped the mining camps Daltrey had spoken about were not all the way in the mountains, but it almost didn't matter at this point. Having come this far, he was not about to turn back. Somehow he had to find a way to release the captives and bring Daltrey down. Deep in his gut, he knew there was only one way to do it. Daltrey would not be coming back to Texas, not because Lex wouldn't try, but because that was the kind of man he was. Wade Daltrey would go down with a bullet through his heart or he wouldn't go down at all.

It was tempting to ease up on the ragged column and pick the colonel off with the Winchester, but it was a temptation Lex would not yield to. He would give the man a chance, even if it meant confronting him one on one, eyeballing each other over a set of gunsights.

For Lex, the law had already bent as far as he was prepared to bend it. He was not a bushwhacker, he was a
Ranger, and that meant there was a proper way to do
things. The only way. The Ranger way.

The column had started to move once again, and
Lex got wearily to his feet. Climbing into the saddle,
he took one more quick look at the sun. In the distance, the mountains were assuming shape now,
resolving out of the purple bruise on the southern
horizon. Already he could see the grooves of ravines,
full of shadow and almost black against their lighter
walls.

They zigzagged through the foothills for the rest
of the afternoon. Daltrey, obviously growing tired,
called a halt more than an hour before sundown.
Lex watched enviously through the glasses as the
raiders built a fire and began to prepare their
evening meal.

The last two nights had been chilly, and at the
higher elevation it would be colder still. Lex knew
that water could freeze even in the middle of summer
in the mountains. They weren't high enough for that
yet, but it would be cold enough to make his bones
ache, his joints stiffen.

As the sun sank in the west, Lex huddled up
against a boulder and wrapped himself in his blankets
to keep warm. He could see the flickering of
Daltrey's fire. Now and then a shadow passed in
front of it. He was too distant to recognize either
Daltrey himself or Eugene, the only two he knew by
name.

The sun disappeared abruptly, almost as if it had
fallen through a hole at the edge of the world. Lex

sat there watching the distant flames, but as the fire died down, he turned his attention to the sky. It was a blue so deep it was nearly black. The stars were almost motionless, barely flickering in the cold air. Once a thin sword slashed across the blackness, as if someone had slashed a curtain, letting in the sun. Even after the meteor was gone, the white line lingered in his field of vision for several seconds.

When it faded, he looked back at Daltrey's camp. The fire was low, but the dim figure of a man on its fire side suggested that someone would stand watch all night and tend the blaze. They weren't going any further that night. It was time to fall back a little, just to make certain he wasn't found by accident.

Lex got back in the saddle. He headed back the way he'd come, finally halting after a mile or so. In the darkness, it had been slow going, and his exhaustion was threatening to overwhelm him. Dismounting, he unsaddled his mount, tethered both horses, and wrapped himself in his blanket once more, finally able to close his eyes, and already shivering from the deepening cold.

When he woke, it was because of something colder still, pressing against his throat. A hand suddenly clamped down over his mouth, pinching his nostrils closed between finger and thumb. He struggled, despite the cold steel pressing on his neck, but without air, he soon lost consciousness, aware only of the knife and of another pair of hands which gripped his shoulders and held him back against the rock so hard he could feel the individual bones in his spine.

When he woke again, it was still dark, but this time it was something he sensed rather than saw. His hands were securely tied behind him, his ankles bound, and a thick cloth wadded over his eyes and knotted at the back of his skull.

He could hear two men, maybe three, speaking in soft voices some distance away. The words were almost inaudible, but he could hear well enough to recognize the guttural Athapascan of a southwestern Indian language, almost certainly Apache, sprinkled with a few Spanish phrases.

He suppressed the urge to call out, thinking it best that they not know he was awake. They might reveal something useful if they thought him unconscious. The Apaches were arguing among themselves, but when the exchanges grew heated, they simply grew more cutting, and hoarse, rather than louder. He could make out nothing but an occasional syllable or two. He recognized *Santa María*, for certain, and one or two other words.

Lex heard footsteps approaching him, faint whispers of soft leather on the rocky ground, then sensed that someone had squatted beside him. He could hear the rasp of someone breathing. He feigned sleep, staying as motionless as he could, letting his head loll against the rock. He resisted the urge to steel himself against the blow of a knife to his chest or throat. It could happen, he knew, but there wasn't a thing he could do about it.

The visitor grunted then, and judging by the sound, straightened up. Lex heard nothing more, as if the Indian had simply turned to vapor and drifted away on the chilly wind. As quietly as he could, keeping the motion to an absolute minimum, he tried his bonds. The rope was securely tied, and there wasn't a chance in hell he could wiggle his hands free. Sawing the rope on the rough edges of the rock behind him would attract attention, self-defeating at least, and at worst fatal.

When he heard no more conversation for better than an hour, he drifted off to sleep. The Indians were being very cautious, and he would learn nothing they didn't want him to know. He needed rest, and if he were to have a chance to escape, he would need every advantage, including stamina.

A hand shook him awake. As far as he could tell from behind the blindfold, it was still the middle of the night. Then fingers grappled with the knot behind his head, and the blindfold came away. It took his eyes some time to adjust. He hadn't realized just how tightly he had been blindfolded, and shooting stars flashed across his field of vision, colored dots swam like tiny fish, gradually dissolving against the dark gray of the sky. It was still early enough that a handful of stars could be seen.

He looked at his captor then. A young Apache, no more than twenty, if that, squatted in front of him. In accented English, he said, "Where are the others?"

"What others?" Lex asked.

"The men who were with you in *Santa María*."

Lex shook his head. "I am alone. There is no one with me."

The Apache lashed out with the flat of his hand, catching Lex on the cheek. It made the skin tingle, and for a few seconds the stars were back. Lex shook off the blow and watched the young warrior closely.

"You were seen in the cantina," the Apache said. "Drinking with the one who wears the old uniform. Where is he?"

"I'm not one of his men," Lex said. He didn't want to give the impression there was any connection between him and Daltrey. It seemed obvious that the Apache was from the *ranchería* Daltrey had savaged and that this young man was out for vengeance. If he thought Lex was one of Daltrey's band, he could expect no mercy.

"I was following him, just like you are."

The Apache snorted. "I am to believe, this, yes?"

"Believe what you want. You asked me and I told you. What else can I do?"

The Apache smiled, then shrugged. "As you wish, señor," he said.

He started to turn away, but swung back so quickly it caught Lex off guard. The blade in his hand swished so close to Lex's face he thought he could feel the tip graze his cheek. The knife then rose high in the air.

Lex closed his eyes for a moment, then watched as the warrior's hand clenched more tightly around the handle of the knife. Despite the near darkness, he could see the young warrior's face clearly. Instead of hatred, the face was glazed with a kind of serenity. Under that, barely noticeable, was a profound sadness, not for what he was about to do, but for those he had recently buried.

Grinding his teeth, the Apache shifted his grasp on the knife once more. Lex saw the tendons in the warrior's forearm tighten and the knife started down. Lex clamped his teeth together, squeezing his jaws as tightly as he could. He was determined to feel nothing, to give this man no satisfaction.

14

"NO!**"**

The shriek cut through the chilly air, and the young warrior stopped the knife in mid-flight. He spun around, his face confused. Lex, too, was baffled. He heard footsteps then, and realized that someone was rushing toward him.

She skidded to her knees in front of Lex, her back to him and her arms held out as if to arrest the descending blade. "Don't," she said. Then, turning to Lex, but still addressing the warrior, she said, "This is the one. The man who saved me."

The young man looked at Lex then, leaning to one side to peer past the woman's shoulder.

"Are you sure?"

"*Sí*, I am sure."

"But he is the one who was drinking with the one who wears the uniform."

"Daltrey," Lex said. "His name is Wade Daltrey."

The warrior looked angry then. "You said you did not know him."

"No, I didn't say that. I said I was not one of his

114

men. That I was not with him. But I know who he is.
I followed him here."

"Why?"

Lex took a deep breath. This was not an easy
question to answer, and he wasn't sure he really
knew. "Because I intend to arrest him."

"You are no Mexicano. You are a gringo. You
cannot arrest him here."

"I'll find a way."

"Why do you want to arrest him?"

"Because he has killed several people in Texas.
Both Apaches, I think, and definitely whites. He's
been causing trouble for a long, long time."

"Then why have you not arrested him before now.
If you know these things about him, he should have
been arrested long ago, no?"

"I don't know, I think many people are afraid of
him. Too afraid to try to arrest him. "

"But you are not afraid?"

"No. I'm not afraid of him."

"You are a soldier?"

Lex shook his head. "No. A Texas Ranger. My
name is Lex Cranshaw."

"I don't know what that is, a Texas Ranger," the
warrior said. "And anyway, I don't know whether I
believe what you say. Why should I believe what you
tell me?"

"I don't suppose you should. But it's the truth,
whether you believe it or not."

The warrior turned to the woman then. "You're
sure this is the man you spoke about?"

She shook her head. "I'm sure."

Lex looked at the woman, leaning forward to see

her through the gloom. "You killed that man, didn't you?" he asked. The woman spun around to look at him. "You crushed his head with a rock, didn't you?"

She gave him a baleful smile. "*Sí*, I killed him. And I would kill him again today, and again tomorrow, and every day for the rest of my life, if I could. I wish I could do that. I saw what he did, what they all did. They killed my father, and they killed my son."

"Why did they take you prisoner?"

She shrugged. "I don't know."

The sky was beginning to turn a lighter gray now, as the sun was rapidly approaching the horizon. Lex could see her face clearly, and the twin streams on her cheeks, glistening in the dim light.

The warrior reached out and pushed her to one side. "You were going to arrest all of these men by yourself?"

"I don't know. I had to follow them, see where they went. I hadn't thought it through any further than that. Once they got where they were going, I would have to find a way. I don't know how, but I would have thought of something. That's what I am paid to do."

"Why did you drink whiskey with him?"

"I wanted to get closer, see what I could learn. I thought maybe he would tell me something. I don't know this country. If I knew where he was going, then maybe I could find him even if I lost him on the trail."

The warrior smiled. "You are not an Apache, that is clear. His trail is easy to follow. The white-eyes are always easy to follow. What did he tell you?"

"He said there was a place where he could sell the

captives as slaves. A mine of some kind. He didn't say where. He also will sell the scalps of the people he killed in your *ranchería*. Fifty American dollars each."

"Always the Mexicans pay money for our hair. And always the Americans come to Mexico and they see that Mexicanos have black hair like Apaches, so they kill Mexicans, too. They kill more Mexicans than they do Apaches." He laughed, but there was no mirth in it.

"Do you know where this mine is that Daltrey was talking about?"

"*Sí*, I know. For many years they have taken my people there to work. They feed them nothing but water and a little corn. And then when they are too weak to work in the mines anymore, they kill them. They prefer women and children though. They are afraid even of the old men. And the young men, they almost never catch. But there are some men there, too. I know this. It is the fault of the Mexicans." He looked closely at Lex. "Do you know why Apaches kill Mexicans with stones?"

Lex shook his head.

"Because we don't want to waste our bullets." He laughed again, this time with a twinkle in his eye. "That is a good joke, isn't it?" he asked. Then, suddenly serious again, he said. "You were following this man Daltrey. Where is he now?"

"He was about two miles ahead of me. Like I said, I don't know the country, so I couldn't stay too far back, but I didn't want to get too close. I am only one man, and there are many of them. Maybe twelve or thirteen. Maybe more. He offered me a job. He may offer jobs to others, too. Although he stays away from the villages, all except Santa María."

"You told me you did not know where they were."

"If I hadn't lied, would I be alive now?"

The Apache nodded. "No. But you did not tell the truth."

"You did not ask me often enough. Is it not true that an Apache will lie, unless you ask him three times, when he must tell you the truth?"

"Yes." The warrior grinned.

"And is it not true that an enemy does not deserve to be told the truth?"

"Am I your enemy?"

"You think so, don't you?"

Again the warrior grinned. "Maybe I was wrong. Maybe you are an Apache after all. Why did you help the woman?"

"Because she needed help."

"But she is an Apache."

"So were the dead children in your *ranchería*."

"So why should that matter to you?"

"Because I don't believe in killing innocent people, especially women and children and old men. I am an officer of the law, and my job is to protect innocent people: Apaches, Comanches, whoever they are. If they break the law, then I will arrest them, and see that they are punished. But if they are innocent, then . . ." Lex trailed off, ending with an eloquent shrug.

"These laws you talk about. They do not apply to Apaches, only to the white-eyes."

"Oh? And why is that?"

"Because it is the white-eyes who make these laws. It is the white-eyes who take our land. It is the white-eyes who kill our people. Even the innocent ones, those who are not warriors, those who are too young even to lift a rifle. And nothing ever happens to these white-eyes. What kind of law is this that only works one way?"

"It's not the law that is wrong, but the men who are supposed to enforce the law."

"Then what difference does the law make? If no one enforces it, then it is the same as if it is not there at all. A law that does not punish those who break it is not a good law."

There was nothing Lex could say. He even agreed. But that was of less immediate concern than what the warrior proposed to do with him. He was about to respond, when the Apache turned away. He was listening intently. "I think . . ." Lex began.

The Apache turned to him with a finger to his lips. Lex heard nothing, but did as he was told. More than a minute later, two more Apaches materialized out of the brush. Their passage was so silent, it seemed almost as if the leaves and branches passed through their bodies.

Both men stared at Lex, but neither said a word. They were older than the other. One bore a jagged scar across one cheek. The young warrior who had been talking to Lex took one of the older men by the arm and led him some distance away. The other Apache moved closer to Lex, squatted down, and stared at him silently.

Lex could no longer see the other two warriors. He knew that he must be the subject of the conversation he had no doubt was taking place. If he had to bet, he'd be willing to wager there was an argument in progress, probably about whether Lex should be killed, possibly about why that hadn't already happened.

It was more than ten minutes before the Apaches returned. The silent one hadn't moved a muscle the entire time. It seemed to Lex that the man's gaze was so intent that his eyes hadn't even blinked.

The young warrior led the way back. He walked over to Lex and squatted in front of him again. "Francisco wants to know if you will help us kill the man Daltrey and his friends."

"Who's Francisco?"

The warrior cocked his head to indicate the man he had been talking to.

"I can't promise that. I want to see to it that he is punished, but I want to try to bring him back to Texas."

"Why?"

"For trial."

"But you know he is guilty. Why do you need a trial?"

"Because that is the way the law works."

"And suppose the law doesn't work? Suppose this man is set free after the trial. Then what?"

Lex took a deep breath. "I don't know."

"Then we will not know where he is. We will not be able to punish him. He will be put on trial for killing white-eyes?"

Lex nodded.

"Not Apaches?"

"Yes, Apaches, too."

"You promise this?"

"Yes."

"But what if he is let go?"

"Then you do what you have to do."

The young warrior pulled his knife again, grabbed Lex roughly by the shoulder and pulled him forward. The Ranger felt the cold steel of the blade on his wrist. A moment later the rope parted.

Lex finally allowed himself to breathe.

THE YOUNG Apache introduced himself as Gerardo. He said he was a cousin of Victorio and that Francisco and the third man, Benito, were brothers and relatives of his by marriage. The woman, whose Spanish name was Juana, was his mother's younger sister.

When the introductions were finished, Lex introduced himself again. "My name's Cranshaw. Lex Cranshaw." He shook hands with all three men. The woman seemed reticent and hung back. Only when Francisco took her by the arm and pulled her forward would she take Lex's offered hand.

"Tell me exactly what happened at the *ranchería*? Lex asked.

Juana shook her head. She backed away and covered her face with her hands.

"It is very hard for her," Francisco said. "As she told you, her son was killed and so was her father. This is not an easy thing to talk about."

"I understand. But we have to know what we're up against. From what I know about this man Daltrey, he is like an animal—bloodthirsty, cruel."

"Like the white-eyes say we are," Benito said. He

didn't smile when he spoke. The other two warriors nodded gravely.

"Why is it so important to know exactly what happened?" Francisco asked. "You saw the *ranchería*. You saw the bodies. The women and children and old men with their scalps taken. What does it matter how it happened?" He glared at Lex. "Or does the white-eyes think maybe the Apaches caused this thing to happen? Does he think maybe that our children attacked this man Daltrey with reeds and tried to take his hair?"

Lex shook his head. "No, of course not. I don't think that. I just want to know exactly what happened. It's important because if I capture him, I want to be able to say exactly what happened. I want to know exactly what crimes he has committed."

"We will say. We will talk at the white-eyes trial. Juana will talk about the dead children."

Lex noticed they mentioned no names, then remembered that Apaches never mention the dead by name, lest their spirits be summoned from the other world.

"I will tell him," Juana said. She moved closer to the small circle of men again, but turned her back, as if she were speaking to the wind. "The men were out hunting. It was mostly women and children and a couple of very old men who were too sick to join the hunt. We were baking mescal. Two of the young boys were on guard, but everything happened so fast that there was no time to run. The men came on their horses and they were shooting at no one, trying to frighten us. I knew then that they wanted to take prisoners, but I did not know why. One man, the one you call Daltrey, had a uniform on and at first I thought it was the white-eyes soldiers. We were off the reservation, we knew that, and I thought they had come to force us to go to the White Mountains."

"Did they say they were soldiers?" Lex asked.

"No. They didn't say anything. And when I saw that the other men did not have on blue coats, I knew they were not soldiers. They circled the camp and chased us. Some got away, but most did not. It happened so fast, and we had no horses. Then they started to shoot again. They shot the old men first, and everyone scattered again. But they chased us down and caught many of us."

She broke down then, choking back her sobs and Lex could see her shoulders quivering as she tried to get her emotions under control once more.

The men waited patiently. Francisco had a fistful of bunch grass and swished it back and forth in the sand. He kept his eyes fixed on Lex, as if trying to gauge his reaction to Juana's words.

Sniffing once or twice, she shook her head, then continued. "They tied us together so that we couldn't run again. They were talking, and I heard them say they were going to take us to Chihuahua and sell us to *Los Mexicanos*. I didn't know then about the mines. Francisco told me about them. The looked at us like we were horses, trying to decide which of us should be sold alive, and which were good only for our hair."

Once more, she turned away, and this time, after standing there for a few seconds, she ran off into the brush. Francisco followed her, after glaring at Lex for a moment.

"I'm sorry," Lex said, knowing it was inadequate and knowing, too, that there was nothing else he could say.

"We want to follow this Daltrey to the mines at Los Altos," Gerardo said.

"Why? It would be easier to take them here," Lex argued, "where we know exactly what we're up against."

"We?" Gerardo asked.

Lex nodded. "I'm not going to let him get away. Not after following him all this way."

"But you say you have no authority here."

"I'll make some of my own," Lex said. "Why not hit them here, before they get to the mine? There will be more men there, maybe Mexican soldiers, too."

Benito spoke for the second time. "Because there are more of our people there, at the mine. We don't want just to save the prisoners the man Daltrey has with him now. We want to release the others, however many there are."

He paused to gauge Lex's reaction, then continued with a shrug. "There are white-eyes without number. Like the grasshopper, they cover the earth in clouds. One more or less makes no difference. But Apaches are few. That is why."

It was an argument with no counter. Lex stayed silent for a long time. When he finally spoke, it was to ask, "How far to the mine?"

"Two days," Gerardo said. "If they go straight there. But I think they will stop at the town of Los Altos. They will want whiskey, and they are too impatient to wait until they get to the mine to sell our

people. They will drink first, maybe take their pleasure with the women. Then they will go to the
mines."

"Are there soldiers in Los Altos?"

Gerardo shrugged. "Sometimes, yes. Not always.
But we cannot ask the soldiers for help. The
Mexicans are like cowards with the Apaches, but
when they are many and we are few, sometimes they
find the courage to fight. If soldiers are at Los Altos,
they will be many."

"I wasn't thinking to ask them for help. I was
afraid they might help Daltrey," Lex said.

"It makes no difference," Benito said. "We will
fight them, no matter how many."

"Shouldn't we get moving? Lex asked.

Benito shook his head, but it was Gerardo who
answered. "We know where they are going. We will
get there first. They take the easy trail. But there are
many other ways."

"Can you get other Apaches?" Lex asked.

"Not now. At the mines, there will be men. Other
traders, who have more courage than this man
Daltrey, have taken warriors to sell to the mines."

"But what about weapons? How can they fight
without weapons?"

Benito held out his hands "These," he said, turning the palms up, then down, then up again and curl-
ing the fingers, "these are weapons. And we will take
guns and knives from the white-eyes. There is a place
in Los Altos where the Mexican soldiers have
weapons."

"An armory?"

Benito shrugged. "I don't know what it is called.

But there are guns and bullets and their long knives there. Many hundreds, even when the soldiers are not there. We will get as many as we need. They are not as good as the guns the blue-coat soldiers have, but they are good enough to kill this man Daltrey and his friends."

"Remember," Lex said, "I want Daltrey alive, if at all possible."

"We will see," Gerardo said.

Francisco came back a moment later, on horseback. Juana was with him. They were leading two additional horses, and Gerardo said, "It is time to go now."

The Apaches waited while Lex saddled his mount, then Benito asked, "Where did you say they were camped?"

Lex pointed, "That way, about two miles ahead. They had a fire. I watched them for an hour or so, then came back to camp here."

Benito nodded. To Francisco, he said, "I will follow them. If something changes, I will come for you at Los Altos."

Francisco shook his head slowly. "Be careful, Benito," he said. Then, without waiting for a response, he wheeled his horse. Gerardo beckoned for Lex to follow, and disappeared into the brush. Lex bulled his way through the tough, thorny undergrowth. Twenty yards later, the brush thinned and Lex found himself heading up a steep slope. Gerardo was at the top, waiting, but Francisco and Juana had already passed out of sight.

Lex pushed the chestnut up the slope, leaning forward against the steep grade. When he reached the top, Gerardo said, "You must try to keep up. Francisco is not happy that you are coming with us. He doesn't trust you."

Lex nodded. "I understand that. I don't know whether I would trust me, either, under these circumstances."

"Don't make a mistake," Gerardo warned. "It will not take much for Francisco to kill you."

"Thanks for the warning. But I don't kill easily, Gerardo."

"But Francisco is no ordinary man."

"All right, I'll be careful. I will do nothing to expose you to danger. But I have to do things my way."

"I understand. Now, we must hurry."

The Apache urged his pony on across the plateau toward a second, less abrupt slope. Lex followed closely, and when they reached the crest, he could see Francisco and Juana far ahead. Gerardo drove his pony unmercifully, and Lex had to struggle to keep pace. His horse was larger and stronger, but it was not used to the kind of terrain, or the unrelenting pressure the pace was exerting.

As he rode, Lex wondered whether he was making a mistake. He wasn't worried about his own safety. If the Apaches had wanted to kill him, his blood would already have clotted in the sand. But he was so close to his quarry. Turning away when the chase was so close to being over seemed like an unnecessary gamble. But he couldn't handle the odds alone, and he could sympathize with the Indians and their desire to free as many of their people as they could.

If the Apaches were right, it could work out to their mutual satisfaction. If not, then he would face the daunting task of finding Daltrey again, and that would not be easy. He wasn't even sure he could do it, with or without help from Gerardo and the others.

They rode all morning and well into the afternoon before stopping for a brief meal. The Apaches were back on their horses before Lex had swallowed the last of his food. He switched mounts to give the chestnut a break, and had to run the roan hard to catch up when Francisco refused to wait for him.

They camped late, without a fire, and the following morning began before sunrise. Lex said a silent prayer, hoping that he could manage the backbreaking pace for one more day. By the time they camped again that night, he wasn't sure he had. His back ached, his legs were cramped, and it felt as if his shoulders were on fire.

"Cranshaw," Gerardo whispered as Lex was drifting off to sleep, "tomorrow morning, you will go into Los Altos."

"How far?" Lex groaned.

"Not far. One hour's ride only."

"Thank God," Lex mumbled.

LOS ALTOS looked strangely prosperous. Through the binoculars, Lex could see several stores, two or three cantinas, a large church, and a number of residences, all arranged around a central square. The Bavispe River meandered past on the eastern edge of the town, its course lined by willows and cottonwoods. Beyond it, the mountains rose sharply.

Several men wearing parts of the uniform of the Mexican army lounged on benches in front of the cantinas. Across the square from the cathedral, a low adobe building, two small field pieces out front, as if to guard the approaches, housed the local army commander. Two sentries stood in front, almost at attention. They were talking to each other while scrutinizing passersby just long enough to decide they posed no threat.

Lex looked at Gerardo, prostrate beside him. "It looks like the army's at home," he said.

The young Apache nodded. "But it will make no difference. If we are quick and careful at the mines, we will be able to free enough people to defeat the soldiers."

"How far is the mining camp from here?" Lex asked.

"Ten miles, a little more maybe. Not far. Francisco and I will go there now while you go into the the village. We will meet back here after dark."

"Be careful, Gerardo," Lex said, clapping the young warrior on the shoulder.

"I am an Apache, Señor Cranshaw. It is you who should be careful." He smiled, and Lex had to laugh at the young man's confidence.

"All right, I'll be careful, too," he said. "What about Juana? Will she go with you?"

Gerardo shook his head. "No. She will stay here and watch what happens. I have glasses like yours, and she will have them to see the village."

A moment later, and Gerardo was gone. Lex backed away from the hilltop and sat in the dirt for a moment. He brushed off his shirt and the front of his jeans, then stood up and walked to his horse. As he mounted, he wondered whether the plan could possibly work. He was anything but confident it would. Three men and a woman taking on a band of cutthroats made for long odds. When you added the possibility of an army unit, no matter how well- or ill-trained, then they got very long indeed.

The Apaches were used to such odds. Lex didn't know whether they fought in spite of them or were so used to being badly outnumbered that they no longer bothered to consider the odds at all.

As he kicked the chestnut into motion, he realized there had been no trace of Daltrey or his men in the village. He hoped none of them were in Los Altos. His presence there would be a dead giveaway for

Daltrey. It could also move the odds from long to impossible. But it was a chance he'd have to take. In order to have any chance of success, it was crucial to know exactly what they were up against. There were enough soldiers visible in the town to suggest that the unit was present in its entirety. According to Francisco, the Mexican soldiers were so nervous about Apaches that they almost never split their forces. The ones left behind would desert rather than risk a confrontation with hostile Indians.

The war between Apaches and Mexicans had been going on for hundreds of years, from the time the first Spaniards pushed north into the American southwest. The tactics of the Spaniards had been cruel beyond belief, and were refined by the Mexicans, who gradually elevated brutality to a fine art. There had been no clear winner, itself amazing, given the disparity in numbers, but attrition was taking its toll. The pressure from white settlers and the American army to the north was squeezing the Apaches in a set of implacable jaws from which only the most reckless could think escape possible, let alone victory.

And yet Cochise, Victorio, Geronimo and many others continued the fight, giving better than they got, outdoing the Mexicans in brutality, outsmarting the Americans at every turn. As their numbers dwindled, they became more elusive, adopting hit-and-run tactics, fighting when there was a chance to inflict damage on the enemy with little risk, running when combat would benefit the enemy more than themselves.

Lex showed the wear and tear of the trail. His

clothes were dusty and he hadn't shaved in several days. He stank, and he knew it. But that was all to the good. The last thing he wanted was to attract attention in Los Altos. His intention was simply to get a meal and a drink, keep his eyes and ears open, and see what he could learn about the size of the army contingent.

If Francisco was right, they were at least a day ahead of Daltrey, maybe even two. This would give them time to reconnoiter the mines, get some idea of the force they would be up against, and plan their attack. One thing Lex and the Apaches agreed on was that they would have one chance and one chance only. If they attacked the mine and failed to free the Indians being held there, Daltrey would get wind of it, and they would lose the chance to free his captives as well.

If they attacked Daltrey and freed the prisoners, security at the mine would be reinforced, reducing, if not eliminating altogether, the opportunity to rescue the Apaches already enslaved. Francisco wanted to take up a position that would enable them to spot Daltrey's approach, begin their attack at the mine and free at least some of the men being held there. They would then have a force large enough to free the rest of the Indians at the mines and hit Daltrey at the same time. This would guarantee that they would not have to deal with the army as well. Or so Francisco argued. Lex was skeptical, but since he had no better plan to offer, he had agreed.

The approach to Los Altos was a straight shot down a gently sloping hill. The sun was high in the sky and the intense heat radiating off the ground made the buildings quiver. Lex headed straight for the center of town, thinking that the most innocent appearance would be the one least noticed. Strange gringos couldn't be too frequent this far south, and one who skulked into town the back way would likely raise a few eyebrows.

He rode directly to a cantina two doors down from the army headquarters. The sentries eyed him as he rode past, and Lex glanced their way just long enough to show that he had nothing to hide. Dismounting and heading into the cantina, he paused on the wooden sidewalk a few moments to take a quick look around the square.

The dank interior of the cantina was full of off-duty soldiers. They clustered around tables and lined the bar, talking among themselves, occasionally bantering with members of other groups. They paid no attention to Lex as he entered. He took a table, and a slender señorita in a blue dress with ruffled sleeves and a full skirt came to take his order.

"Una cerveza, por favor," Lex said.

She smiled. "I speak English, señor," she said. Laughing, she walked toward the bar, got a bottle of beer and a glass, and returned to his table. "You would like something to eat, señor?"

Lex nodded. "You have chicken?"

"Sí."

"Good, some chicken and a bowl of rice and black beans, please."

"How would you like your chicken, señor?"

"Cooked," Lex said.

She looked puzzled for a moment, then, when she saw his grin, she smiled. "Of course, señor. But how?"

"Any way but boiled, señorita."

"I take care of it," she said.

Lex watched her negotiate her way through the maze of admiring glances and casual hands until she disappeared behind the bar and through a door into what Lex took to be the kitchen.

The beer was warm, as he'd expected. Ice was a precious commodity in this part of Mexico, all but unavailable except in the winter months, when it could be lugged down from the higher elevations. Even in summer, water often froze overnight in the Sierra Madres, but in the valleys it stayed warm, and the people used ice only when available and then only for essentials. The foods were all dried for preservation rather than frozen.

The beer was good, but he didn't recognize the brand. He traced the name of the brewery etched into the glass just below the neck, and realized it was of Mexican origin. The taste was lighter than that of the thick, dark German beers so common in Texas.

While he waited for his meal, he watched the soldiers. They seemed relaxed, even friendly. If they were worried about an imminent attack on the mines or the village, there was no evidence of it.

Two more soldiers came in, looked around and, seeing that the only table with room was the one at which Lex sat, they came over diffidently. Without waiting for them to ask, Lex nodded at the chairs and said, "*Siéntense, amigos.*"

They smiled and took a seat.

The waitress was coming back now, once more running the gauntlet, balancing a tray on one hand and cradling another beer in the other.

She set the tray on the table and said, "I brought another beer, señor. I thought you would need it to wash down the rice and beans. They are a little dry, I think."

"Thank you," Lex said. "How much do I owe you?"

"Two pesos, señor. If you only have American dollars, I can change them for you."

Lex nodded, fished a dollar out of his pocket, and handed it to her. Looking at the two soldiers, he said, "Can I buy you gents a drink?"

The taller and older of the two smiled broadly, showing the gaps between his teeth. "*Sí, gracias, señor,*" he said. "Tequila."

"*Dos tequilas, señorita,*" Lex said. The girl frowned, but didn't argue.

In Spanish, Lex asked the men their names. The tall one, answering in English, said he was called Pedro, then introduced the shorter man as Domingo.

"How do you like the army?" Lex asked, as he started on the chicken. He realized it was too much food for him, an entire roasted chicken, and he took a knife from the tray and cut it down the middle, then offered half to the soldiers.

"*Gracias, señor,*" Pedro said, reaching for the chicken and holding it in the air while Lex scooped his rice and beans from their bowl onto the chicken dish, then pushed the bowl toward Pedro.

"It's all right. It is better than pushing a plow, but I miss my family. Sometimes they come with me, sometimes not. This time, not."

"Are they far?" Lex asked.

Pedro shrugged. "Five hundred miles."

"A long way."

"*Sí*, a long way. And you are a long way from home, too, are you not, señor?"

Lex nodded. He ripped a leg from the half-chicken and started to tear meat off it before answering. "A very long way," he said.

Pedro munched on a piece of chicken, and Domingo snatched at a wing, to tear strips of crackling skin free. Neither of the soldiers spoke while Lex continued to eat his rice and beans. The waitress was back with two glasses of tequila, set them in front of the two soldiers, and disappeared into the crowd again.

"What are you doing here, señor?" Pedro asked. "Are you a prospector?"

"Just passing through, is all."

"Prospecting?"

"No."

"I didn't think so. I didn't see a pick or shovel on your horses. Those are fine animals, señor."

"Thank you."

There was a long pause while Pedro finished his piece of chicken. Lex sipped at his beer, wondering why Pedro was so curious.

Setting the bones in the empty bowl, Pedro turned to Domingo, who was busy tearing meat from between the bones of the wing. It looked as if he were afraid to break the bones, and worried the meat free with a fingernail just enough to grab it between his fingertips, then tear it loose.

"Did you see any Apaches in the mountains, señor?" Pedro asked.

Lex shook his head. "No, thank goodness."

"So, what *are* you doing in Los Altos, señor?"

"Just stopped on the way north, is all."

"But you came in from the north, señor. Perhaps your compass is broken, eh?"

Suddenly, he held a pistol in his hand. His thumb rested on the hammer, its nail glistening with chicken grease. "Maybe you should talk to Major Valdivar. Maybe he can tell you which way is north, eh?"

For a second, Lex was tempted to go for his gun. But a look around the gloomy cantina convinced him it would be suicide.

He wiped his lips with a napkin, took a last sip of beer, and stood up. "All right," he said. "Let's go."

"Thank you for making no trouble, señor," Pedro said.

"And thank you, too, for the chicken and the tequila," Domingo added, tossing off his drink in a single swallow.

"What's this all about?" Lex asked.

"I don't know, señor. But Major Valdivar will tell you, I think."

He smiled, and it seemed genuine.

17

MAJOR GOZAGO Valdivar sat behind a rickety-looking desk. The small office that served as his headquarters was dusty, cramped, and stank a little of perspiration. His graying hair was the least bit unkempt, and his uniform was frayed at the cuffs. To make up for the lack of elegance of his surroundings, the Major had a decidedly imperial manner.

"You are here on business, señor?" he asked, folding his hands over his substantial stomach.

Lex shook his head. "No, Major. Just passing through."

"That is not what I hear, señor."

"Well, I don't know who could tell you my business except me, Major. I don't know anyone in Los Altos."

"Passing through from where, señor?" The major smiled broadly.

"Magdalena."

"And what was your business there? Or were you just passing through Magdalena as well, señor?"

"No. I was there looking up an old friend."

"Who?"

"Don Vincenzo de la Granada."

"And did you find him?" Valdivar rubbed his chin, a little uncertain now. Such a name was not one used lightly. Lex was fortunate that he had met Granada at his father-in-law's hacienda on one or two occasions. Don Vincenzo was a former governor of Sonora Province, and had friends in all the right places. It was doubtful that he would remember Lex, but it was just as doubtful that Valdivar would check. The major would not want to take the chance that Lex was telling the truth. To imprison a friend of Don Vincenzo on a whim was not something that would help his career if, in fact, he had one left after so grievous a breach of Mexican hospitality.

Still, it was apparent that he had not made the decision to arrest Lex on his own. Someone had put a bug in his ear. And there was only one possibility. But how had Daltrey known he was in Los Altos?

"Major, if you don't mind, I'd like to take care of my horses. We can talk more about this later. Maybe I can—"

"Señor, I don't think you understand. This is not some hospitable chat we are having. That is a good word, no? Chat? I learned this word from an English gentleman who was passing through last year." This time his smile was ear to ear. "It seems many gringos, and even Inglís, pass through Los Altos, but no one bothers to stay. Maybe our climate is not to your liking. Too hot, maybe?"

"Maybe," Lex said. "But if this is not a chat, what is it, then?"

"We will talk about it in the morning, señor. Tonight you will enjoy our humble hospitality, humn?"

"Am I under arrest?"

"Nothing so crude as that, señor. Let us just say that you are forcibly invited to partake of our famous Mexican generosity to strangers."

"For what reason, Major?"

Valdivar shrugged. "Because it is our way, señor. Because it pleases us to know that you do not have to sleep on the ground, at least for this one night. Who knows what might happen to you otherwise. Scorpions, rattlesnakes, *los banditos*. A thousand perils for the unwary stranger, señor."

Valdivar stood up. He clapped his hands, and two men entered the office. Pedro and Domingo were back. One took up a position on either side of Lex, standing at attention, waiting for their commander's next order.

Valdivar tilted his head, as if to get a different perspective on his reluctant guest. Then, with a nod, he stepped past Lex and on out into the street. "This way, señor," he called back over his shoulder.

Valdivar gradually increased the distance between himself and his prisoner, then disappeared into a small building across the square. The two guards followed at a leisurely pace, Domingo occasionally prodding Lex in the ribs with a handgun to make certain he didn't lag behind.

They entered the small building, one guard leading the way, the other waiting for Lex to precede him. The smell was overwhelming. It took Lex a moment to place the miasma of human waste and damp straw. It smelled like a stable that had been home to a dozen victims of dysentery. Valdivar stood to one side, a scented hankie over his nose. When he spoke, his voice was muffled and sounded as if his nose were tightly pinched between hidden thumb and forefinger.

Three cells lined the back wall. Two were full, half a dozen peasants or more crammed into spaces fit only for one. The third, the one in the middle, was empty. Its rusty iron door yawned open, and Valdivar bowed before gesturing for Lex to enter. "Inside, please, señor," he said, flashing one more smile. "I am sorry about the smell, but . . ." He shrugged.

The guards stood by while Valdivar closed the door and locked it, then hung the keys on a wooden peg mounted high on the wall across from Lex's cell. "I will be back to see you in the morning, señor," the major said. "Perhaps by then you will remember why you are here, eh?"

There was no point in arguing, so Lex just stood at the door, his hands curled around the bars, watching the major closely. Valdivar tossed an off-handed salute, then went out. The two guards followed him, closing the wooden door to the cell block.

Lex shook his head. Somehow, he had to manage to get out, but it would not be easy, and he had to consider the possibility that the soldiers would be waiting for him to do just that. But he couldn't stay here, not with Wade Daltrey so close. He had to find a way out. What he would do then, he didn't know. Valdivar had taken his weapons, and his horses were God only knew where.

The stench was overpowering, but there was nothing he could do about it except try to breathe through his mouth. He moved toward the back wall, looked up at the window, and noticed that there was no glass, only bars. It would be cold during the night, and they had neglected to give him a blanket. Or was it neglect?

He looked at the cells on either side of him and noticed that none of the other prisoners had blankets. Some were already sleeping, lying against the walls, half buried in the nauseating straw.

Lex scraped a clean place against the base of the wall and sat down with his back against the damp stone. There was nothing to do but wait for dark and hope that something would occur to him. At the moment, it didn't seem too likely a prospect. But he was tired and sleep wouldn't hurt, if only it were possible.

He closed his eyes, trying to block out the stink, and to ignore the mumbling from the cells on each side of him. Once, something moved in the straw, probably a mouse, he thought, and suppressed a shiver, hoping it was nothing larger.

It was well past dark when he woke, after fitful sleep that left him somewhat rested, but no more comfortable. His bones ached, and his back felt as if he'd been kicked by a mule. The damp stone had given him a cramp. The air in the cell was chilly now, and he was almost grateful. The fetid stench was less aggressive because of the cold.

The other prisoners were sprawled on the floors of their cells, a tangle of dirty laundry and untamed hair. Half hidden by shadows, they were a shapeless mass of anonymous offenders whose only crime, in all likelihood, was their poverty. That was the way it went in Mexico. The army was an instrument of the landowners, and the peasants had to scrape and claw at the barren ground to find enough food to keep body and soul together. But that was not his concern at the moment.

Getting to his feet, he felt awkward, the stiffness in his joints hampering his movement. He stretched, then did some bends and twists, trying to loosen his cold-stiffened muscles. When he felt a little closer to human, he walked to the cell door. He couldn't actually see the keys where they hung on the wall opposite him, but he thought he remembered where they were. It didn't matter whether they were still there because there was no way he could reach them, but knowing they were there would give him the hope that the key would turn in the lock once more, that he would not spend the rest of his life in this miserable hole. It was scant comfort, but it was all he had.

Moving to the back wall, he jumped to catch one of the bars, then dug his toes into the rough stone, hauling himself up to hang on with one arm while he tried the bars with his free hand. They were secure, cemented into the center of a thick wall. It would take a pick, or a stick of dynamite, to get them loose. Since he had neither, he faced the reality that he was wasting his time and dropped to the floor with a sigh of resignation.

There was no way out of the cell. His only chance would be to make a break for it in the morning, if they brought him back to see Valdivar. He doubted the major would bother to show up at the cell, since there was no real opportunity for him to act grandiose, at least not with a hankie over his nose. Lex had seen the cell, and there was nothing else Valdivar could show him, certainly nothing worth standing by to gloat over. The stench alone was enough of a deterrent to a second visit from the major. If Valdivar was going to talk to him again as he had said, then Lex would be brought to him.

It would be a simple matter to disarm one of the guards. If he were quick enough, he could get the drop on the second. But then what? Taking the guards prisoner and offering to exchange them for his guns and horses almost certainly wouldn't work. Valdivar would tell him to shoot the soldiers. They were nothing to him. On the other hand, if he ran, how long could he last without horses and weapons?

Juana, he knew, was in the hills above the town. But assuming he could find her, what good what it do? Even if she had a rifle she would have only one horse. The more he thought about it, the bleaker his prospects seemed. But sitting there like a vegetable was no help at all, so he kept turning possibilities over in his mind, the way a child examines a shiny stone pulled from the bottom of a creek.

Lex was getting restless. The anticipation of his escape attempt was worse than the risk itself, and he tried to push it out of his mind.

As he sat there, staring at the few stars he could see through the tiny window, a sound caught his attention. For a moment, he thought one of the men in an adjacent cell had said something to him. He listened intently, but the sound was not repeated.

Then he heard the squeak of a hinge. He moved to the corner of his cell, his eyes fixed on the front door. Another tiny squeak pierced the silence, then he could see a rectangle of light appear in the wall.

The light was blocked for a moment, and the figure of a man appeared, then disappeared as the man moved inside the jailhouse.

"Señor?" It was a hoarse whisper. "Señor Cranshaw?"

"Here," Lex hissed. "Who is it?"

"Gerardo, señor. Where are the keys?"

"On the wall, to the left of the door." He squeezed up against the bars then, barely able to see the young Apache. He heard a momentary jingle, then Gerardo's fingers closed over the loose keys and squeezed them into silence.

The Apache found the lock quickly, inserted the key and ground the lock open. Lex pushed the door back and stepped out. Something prodded him in the stomach and he reached for it, his hands closing over the butt of a handgun.

"Quickly, señor," Gerardo whispered. Then the Apache darted outside. Lex was right on his heels. He nearly tripped over the prostrate form of the night guard. Glancing down as he moved past, he saw the gaping wound under the Mexican's chin, and the pool of shiny blackness slowly spreading on the stone sill. For a second, Lex saw a handful of stars reflected in the blood, then Gerardo pulled him by the arm, and tugged him along the front of the jail-house and around a corner.

"How did you . . . ?"

"Not now, señor. There is no time."

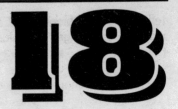

FRANCISCO AND Benito were waiting on
the edge of town. Lex was surprised to
see his horses standing, saddled and
ready, among the ragged cottonwoods by the river.
Juana, a rifle cradled across her saddle, smiled when
she saw him.

Lex looked at Gerardo. "How did you get my
horses?"

"It wasn't easy, señor. But . . . " He shrugged.

"How did you know what . . . ?"

"Juana saw everything. We had to wait until after
dark to begin, and there were many steps. But it is
done, and that is the important thing, Señor
Cranshaw, is it not?"

Lex nodded. "Yes, it is."

Francisco stepped forward then, out of the shadows. He carried Lex's new Colt and Winchester 73.

"Where . . . ?"

Francisco grunted. He shoved the weapons into
Lex's hands. Lex strapped on the gunbelt, then
walked to the chestnut to shove the Winchester into
its boot. He looked at Gerardo then.

The young warrior smiled sheepishly. "The

Mexican officer has no further need of them," he said.

Lex started to ask another question, but Francisco interrupted. "There is no time. We have to be at the mines by sunrise."

Without waiting for an answer, he climbed into the saddle, a small Mexican affair, ornamented with silver, and motioned for Gerardo and Benito to do the same. Lex was the last one in the saddle, and Franciso was already in motion by the time Lex clapped his knees against the chestnut's sides.

They moved along the riverbank, keeping to the narrow strip of grass between the brush and the water's edge. Lex glanced back once, but the small sliver of moon cast so little light that Los Altos was nothing more than a dark gray mass in the shadows.

Francisco led the way up and out of the river valley as soon as it was safe to do so. They followed the bed of a dry wash up into rocky ground, then reached a tableland. In the darkness, it was difficult to see where they were headed, but Francisco knew, and, for the time being, he was in charge.

They rode for three hours, the horses moving ahead at little more than a fast walk. It was apparent the Apaches were not afraid of pursuit, either because they had such confidence in themselves, or because they knew the soldiers would be rudderless without Major Valdivar.

Benito dismounted first, then Gerardo. Juana, too, slipped from her horse. A few yards ahead, an arroyo cut across the tableland, and the dismounted Apaches tugged their horses toward it, then down into it. Lex started to dismount, but Francisco said,

"No. You come with me. I want to show you the mining camp. The others have already seen it, but in the morning there will be no time for you to learn. We will have to strike quickly. It is important that you know what you have to do."

Lex noticed that Franciso had no doubt of his cooperation. He was tempted to object, but realized that the Apache was right. Francisco knew the terrain, and he was the most experienced warrior among the four men. It was only fitting that he command. That was always the way the Apaches went to war. Each man followed if he chose. If he did not, for whatever reason, the others assumed that he knew what was best for him.

Lex wondered whether there would be fewer wars if all men were free to decide for themselves whether to fight. But there was no way to know, and there was no way men would be given such a choice. Not in the foreseeable future, anyway, so it was one of those meaningless philosophical questions with which Lex filled the long night hours.

He followed the Apache for another mile, reining in when Francisco held up a hand. "We must go on foot, now," the warrior said. Dismounting, he took a lariat from the back of his small saddle, and draped it over his shoulder. Then he gave a second rope to Lex. Finally, he loosed a pair of canvas bags from the back of his mount, draped them over his broad shoulders, and waved for Lex to hurry.

Lex slipped from the saddle and used the reins to hobble the chestnut. Francisco waited impatiently, then moved ahead on foot. Lex followed as close behind as he dared in the dim light. The footing was relatively good, but small cholla and prickly pear cactuses clawed at his boots, and twice he tripped and fell headlong. Even with his burden, Francisco had no trouble at all, and when Lex climbed back to his feet after the second fall, he saw the Apache grinning at him.

After about three hundred yards, Francisco stopped, pulled Lex by the arm as he dropped to his knees, then gestured for Lex to crawl. The Apache led the way. They were moving into a rocky area, and the boulders made going difficult. Lex threaded his way among the huge stones, feeling smaller ones under his palms and knees. Suddenly the ground sloped sharply downward, and Lex sprawled on his stomach, reaching for ground that wasn't there.

They were overlooking a box canyon, and Lex could see at least three fires, one large one, burning in the middle of an empty square. Beyond the large fire, a three-sided palisade of stakes, a large gate in the center, enclosed the base of the back wall of the canyon. In the far corner, a waterfall dropped over the high cliff, catching the firelight and glittering like liquid gold as it plunged nearly a hundred and fifty feet to the canyon floor.

The two smaller fires, one on either side of the mouth of the canyon, were surrounded by the forms of sleeping men. Francisco tugged on Lex's sleeve, then pointed toward the palisade. "The Apaches are kept in there," he whispered.

"How many guards?" Lex asked.

"Many. Maybe twenty. Maybe more than twenty."

"How can we possibly free the captives against that kind of force?" Lex asked.

Francisco pointed to the back wall of the canyon.

"I will climb down behind the fence. I have guns and knives, a few, but enough. You will lower them to me. Then, in the morning, when the guards open the fence, we will escape. You and Gerardo and Benito will be up here with long guns. You can kill many of them before they know what is happening. With the gate open, the man Daltrey will be here tomorrow, and . . . "

"How do you know that?" Lex interrupted.

"I know it. It is so."

Lex heaved a sighed. "Go on, Francisco," he said.

"When the man Daltrey comes, he and his people will come into the canyon, and . . . "

"But he'll realize there's something wrong when he doesn't see the soldiers."

"He will see soldiers, señor. But they will not be Mexican soldiers. They will be *Apache* soldiers." We will wear the uniforms. It will not fool him for long, but it will fool him long enough for him to come all the way into the canyon. Once that happens, then we will close the canyon behind him. He will not be able to escape. And we will free all our people, those already here and those with the man Daltrey."

"It's very risky, Francisco."

"For an Apache, señor, life is always risky. That is what it means to be an Apache. It is the only way. If we attack from the mouth of the canyon, the imprisoned ones cannot help. If we wait until the man Daltrey gets here, there will be too many guns for us. We must get some of the Mexican soldiers' guns, and we have to do that quickly, when the sun comes up."

"What if they see you going down the wall?"

"They will not look at the wall, señor. They are

always drunk and sleeping. They rely on the fence to keep the Apaches in."

"All right. When do you want to do this?"

"Now, señor. Now. This way," he said, backing away from the edge of the canyon and leading Lex on a frightening walk of the perimeter.

The sloping ground underfoot made the Ranger feel as if he were about to slide out into thin air. Sand slipped from under the soles of his boots, and once he kicked a rock hard enough that it cracked against another. Francisco stopped then, waited for him to catch up, and grabbed him by the shoulder. "You must be quiet, señor," he said.

Lex nodded, feeling a little embarrassed. Francisco moved so silently and so easily that Lex couldn't even hear him two yards ahead. The Ranger felt as if he were a child learning a man's craft.

They reached the back wall of the canyon without further mishap, and Francisco dropped his bags and rope to the ground. Lex watched as the Apache uncoiled the rope, fashioned a secure loop in one end, then checked the entire length for fraying or other weak spots. When he was satisfied, he slipped the loop over his head, pulled it down and tightened it under his armpits, leaving his arms free.

"You will have to hold very tight, señor," he said, handing the rest of the rope to Lex.

"You want me to lower you down?"

"No, just keep the rope tight. I will climb down, but if I slip . . . " He nodded.

"You trust me to do that?" Lex asked.

"Who else is there to trust, señor? We are the only ones here."

"All right. When you get to the bottom, jerk the rope twice. I'll pull it up and lower the bags."

"No. I will need the rope in the prison, señor. You will have to let it fall."

"Too much noise, Francisco. You don't want to take the chance. I'll tie it to the end of the other rope. When I lower the bags, it will come down, too."

"As you wish, señor."

"There's no chance the prisoners can just climb up? We can stay here and hold the ropes to make certain . . ."

"Many of them are very weak, señor. They are not given much food, and some are sick. They can kill Mexicans on the ground, but they do not have the strength to climb up the ropes. This is the only way."

Lex tied one end of the rope securely around a large boulder, then moved forward with the remainder coiled in his hands. The Apache was already at the lip of the canyon wall. He dropped to his knees and Lex darted forward. Clapping the Apache on the shoulder, he said, "Good luck, Francisco."

The Apache nodded. Then he flashed Lex a grin. "Apaches don't need luck, señor. It is the Mexicans who need luck. And tomorrow morning, that luck will run out. After you lower the bags, go back to Gerardo and the others. They know what to do in the morning."

Lex watched as Francisco flattened himself on the edge of the canyon wall, then swung out and down. For a moment, his hands were visible on the edge of the rimrock. Then they were gone. The rope payed out slowly as the Apache climbed down the sheer face of the rock.

Lex listened for a dislodged stone, any sound that might alert a guard, but he heard nothing. He kept his eyes on the sleeping soldiers at the far end of the canyon. They were just blue and white blurs around the fire, barely distinguishable as men.

The descent seemed to take forever. More than once, Lex was tempted to creep to the edge to look down into the blackness and make sure that Francisco was all right. But he resisted, instead settling in with his heels against a slab of stone, his hands slowly paying out the lariat.

He thought the signal would never come. His back was tense, his shoulders on fire from the tension. Finally, he felt the rope wiggle, then again. He relaxed his grip, uncrimping his fingers as he felt the slack in the rope, then got to his feet and grabbed the two bags full of weapons. Working quickly, he knotted the second rope around the tether holding the two bags together. He looped the other end of the new rope around a rock next to the one where Francisco's anchor was secured. Then, unknotting the first rope, he looped it loosely around the end of the second, tied a slip knot, and moved to the edge of the rim.

He let the bags dangle from the end of one arm, then slowly payed out the rope. The bags were heavy, but he didn't want to risk letting them slap against the wall. Unlike Francisco, the bags might dislodge loose stone, making enough noise to rouse one of the sleeping guards. He wanted to believe that all of them were drunk, as Francisco said, but there was always that one man who did the unexpected.

The weight of the ropes added to the strain on his

shoulders as he lowered the freight. Once, the bags bumped an outcropping. He heard a crack a few seconds later, as a broken stone fell to the canyon floor. He held his breath, but nothing happened.

Working more quickly now, he payed out the rest of the rope, feeling that he had dodged a bullet. He knew enough about odds to believe that he would not get the chance to dodge a second one.

Then, an eternity later, he felt the rope go slack. Once more, two tugs signaled that the bags were on the ground. Two more tugs told him the rope could be pulled up. He started hauling it in, hand over hand, until he had it coiled at his feet.

Now there was nothing to do but join the others and wait for morning.

And maybe say one little prayer.

19

WHEN DAWN came, Lex was in position in a cluster of boulders over the rear wall of the canyon. Gerardo was on the left wall and Benito on the right. He couldn't see either of them, but knew they had taken up positions that would give them a clear view of the open area between the mouth of the canyon and the palisade gate.

For the plan to succeed, timing was everything, and Lex grew tense as the sky turned light gray. He searched the rimrock for signs of either of the Apaches, but saw nothing. Nor did he really expect to. He could see the soldiers beginning to stir in the canyon below him, and three or four men were already up and about, adding wood to the fires from a huge stack of pre-cut timber that lined the base of the left wall.

Juana was two miles away, on high ground over-looking the approach to the canyon. She had a mirror, and would signal as soon as Daltrey's men passed in front of her. Lex could see the Apaches below him. Their clothes were ragged, just strips of gray in the shadows behind the palisade, but they were ready. Crouched on either side of the gate, several men appeared to be whispering among themselves. The women and children, by far the greater number, huddled in one corner. Some, he was sure, were inside one of the mine shafts, where they would be out of harm's way.

Everything was ready. Now all they needed was a little bit of luck. The sky continued to brighten, and Lex watched as two of the soldiers trundled a large cauldron, on a metal frame with wooden wheels, into position over a fieldstone fire pit. They lit the fire, added some kindling, then started to pour water from wooden buckets they ferried back and forth from the creek that wound along the left wall of the canyon.

One of them then lugged a heavy sack, apparently burlap, to the cauldron, slit it with a bayonet, then hoisted the sack to the lip of the cauldron. Lex could see the contents, what looked like corn, cascade through the slit, sending up a plume of gray dust as it disappeared into the water.

It looked as if the gate to the pen would not be open until the food was ready. One of the soldiers stood by the cauldron with a wooden paddle the size of an oar, and stirred the contents from time to time. He was not particular about where the paddle touched between stirrings, as often as not leaning on it as if he were a wizened old man with a cane too large for him. The broad blade was in the dirt beside his feet until it was time for another stir.

The flames licked up along the sides of the cauldron, and the other fires in the camp were being stoked, sending columns of smoke into the air. The camp was rudimentary, and for that Lex was grateful.

A pair of large tents had been pitched beside the mouth of the canyon, on the right side, and two wooden shacks, not large enough for barracks, probably storage of some kind, perhaps for weapons, ammunition, and tools, sat on the left, between the firewood and one end of the compound palisade.

There were few places for the soldiers to hide inside the canyon. They could, of course, run through the open gate and into the mines, but in order to reach the shafts, they would have to fight their way through Francisco and the prisoners. That seemed unwise, and rather unlikely. Lex couldn't imagine the soldiers willingly allowing themselves to be trapped and at the mercy half a hundred starving and vengeful Apaches, even if most of them were women and children. When Lex remembered the shattered skull of Juana's would-be rapist, he shuddered involuntarily, and knew the only place the soldiers would run was out of the canyon mouth and into the flatlands beyond.

He was beginning to wonder whether it might not be wiser for him to change positions, moving toward the canyon mouth, where he could look down into the enclosed area or out into the flats. His height advantage would give him a clear shot in either direction, and there was little cover other than scattered brush and boulders outside the canyon. But it was too late for that, now. The last thing he wanted to risk was alerting the soldiers below that someone was watching them.

The gruel in the cauldron was boiling now, large bubbles of thick-skinned and glutinous yellow muck expanding on the surface and bursting with nearly audible pops, emitting clouds of gray steam into the chilly morning air. It was almost time.

Two of the soldiers approached the cauldron, slipping the straps of canvas slings over their shoulders. It took Lex a moment to realize the slings contained wooden bowls. Another pair moved to open of the sheds, opened the doors, and brought out a two-wheeled wooden cart. One man faced away from the cart and bent slightly to grab the wooden handles, then straightened and started toward the cauldron, while the other closed the shed again. The cart contained several buckets.

As soon as the cart reached the cauldron, the second man grabbed two of the pails by their bails. The man pulling the cart set it down and grabbed another pair of buckets. Both men dunked the pails into the gruel and hauled them out, the boiled corn clinging to its sides and spattering the outside of the cauldron, then the ground as they were placed into the cart.

The drayman positioned himself between the handles of the cart again, bent and straightened, then lurched toward the gate in the palisade. The rusty barbed wire on top of the fence shook in the wind, and shuddered as one of the two sling-bearers began to unlock the gate.

Lex tensed, slid the safety off his Winchester, and watched the soldiers in the open. He was not going to shoot first. Francisco had the first move. If he could overpower the four men without a shot being fired, their task would be made that much simpler.

The gate swung back, and the man hauling the cart staggered toward it. The two sling bearers, with drawn pistols stood to one side, waiting for him to get all the way inside. The fourth man, also holding a revolver, followed him in. The rest of the detachment, apparently used to the enforced docility of their charges, paid no attention to the labor of their comrades, as if they could not believe trouble was possible.

And Francisco sprang. He grabbed one of the sling-bearers, dragged him to the ground at the same moment the crouching Apaches swarmed over the remaining men.

A gunshot cracked then, and one of the Apaches staggered back, a bright stain on the front of his ragged gray shirt.

The soldiers out in the compound started to scurry around, shouting to their companions. The pyramided rifles, bayonets fixed, around the central fire, were passed out hurriedly as more gunfire erupted behind the palisade.

Lex sighted on his first target as gunshots cracked from either flank. Gerardo and Benito were opening up. Two men fell to the ground as Lex squeezed the trigger for the first time. He saw his man go down on one knee, turning his face to the rimrock before falling on his side.

The firing was furious now. Several of the soldiers, led by the only man in full uniform, apparently an officer of some kind, started toward the palisade, their rifles extended in front of them, the bayonets glittering brightly in the early sunlight.

The palisade gate was still open, but from his location, Lex could see that the Apaches were back against the fence on either side of it. They had four more guns now, but were patiently holding their ground. A volley at close quarters, even from the out-moded Mexican rifles, would be deadly.

Lex fired again, then a third time, picking off two more soldiers who seemed confused and uncertain as to what they should be doing. They had been running back and forth like shuttles on a loom, toward the mouth of the canyon then back toward the palisade.

The advancing soldiers were almost to the gate now. Lex did a quick count—ten, not many. But the Indians inside the palisade were weak from hunger, probably no match for the army men in hand to hand combat. Lex looked for another target, but the soldiers had all scattered now, except for the infantry advancing on the yawning gate.

He turned his Winchester on them just as Gerardo fired. The officer in the lead stumbled and fell to one knee, his blue coat now sprouting a bright red flower in the center of its back. He doubled over for a moment, and when he straightened up, his white pants were splashed with blood. From that distance, they looked to Lex like they had been embroidered with rosebuds. The soldiers behind him stopped in their tracks, uncertain whether to continue on or wait for him to regain his composure.

Glancing to his right, Lex saw Benito running along the rimrock, back toward the mouth of the canyon. Lex got to his feet and raced after the Apache. Suddenly, Francisco charged out of the gate, a horde of ragged captives behind him. The officer, still on one knee, raised a hand, but before he could call for fire, Francisco reached him. The warrior shot him in the face at point blank range and the officer sprawled on his back.

When their commander fell, the soldiers broke ranks. Some dropped their rifles and ran, others turned tail, looking over their shoulders and clinging to their rifles but making no attempt to fire them.

Gerardo fired rapidly from the rimrock, emptying his rifle at the fleeing men. Benito was no longer visible, and when Lex reached the mouth of the canyon, he saw the Apache halfway down the precipitous slope. Several of the running Mexicans burst through the mouth of the canyon and one or two were trying to rally their comrades, shouting for them to stop and use their weapons.

One of them spotted Benito and shouted. He pointed up the slope at Benito, who had his hands full with his descent. One of the soldiers raised his rifle and Lex dropped to one knee, aimed and fired, all in one continuous motion. He saw the soldier take a step back, and thought for a moment he had missed.

The soldier clutched at his chest then, and his rifle fell to the ground. He staggered another step backward. One of his comrades went to his aid while two more brought their rifles to their shoulders and aimed up the slope. Lex fired again, jerked the lever and chambered another shell. Too late, he saw the puff of smoke and heard the crack of the long gun.

Benito stumbled, and Lex couldn't tell whether he'd been shot or had simply dived out of the way. He watched anxiously for a second, then saw Benito spread both arms to claw at the ground as he skidded several feet over the slippery sand. When he was able to arrest his slide, the Apache scrambled behind some boulders for a moment, then continued on downhill.

Lex fired again, and this time the soldiers ran. They were running away from the canyon, following the trail toward the creek which would take them back toward Los Altos. They had to be stopped. If they reached Daltrey, the trap would be useless.

Lex shouted to Benito, and pointed in the direction of the running men. Four soldiers were rapidly approaching the brush along the creek. He aimed and fired, saw one fall, but his next shot was hurried, and missed, kicking up a puff of dust inches from the heels of his target.

Benito opened up, and a second soldier fell. A horrendous howling suddenly exploded below, and Lex saw the freed Apaches pouring through the canyon mouth. Benito yelled to them, and pointed out the fleeing soldiers.

Lex saw Gerardo skidding down the slope on the far side, also yelling to those below to stop the fugitives. Instinctively, Lex looked toward the hilltop where Juana was hidden, but saw nothing to indicate that Daltrey was approaching.

The freed prisoners seemed energized by their freedom and spurted forward, rapidly closing the gap between themselves and their prey.

Several sported bayonets taken from the captured Mexican rifles, and the blades glinted in the sunlight as the Apaches brandished them overhead. The howling curdled Lex's blood, and he suppressed a shiver as he started down the slope.

The soldiers made it into the brush, but Francisco was less than thirty yards behind the trailer now, and closing fast. It would be just a matter of time before the two fugitives were brought to bay. Benito joined the chase, but Gerardo stayed behind. When he reached the bottom, he sprinted toward Lex, who still had fity feet to go before he reached the bottom.

"I better stay with you, señor. My people are in no mood to be kind to white-eyes," he said, as Lex skidded the last few feet, lost his footing and landed on his rump. The Apache grinned at him then. "You are not used to our mountains, señor. I can see that."

Lex started to answer when a single gunshot cracked in the brush, then a chilling scream seemed to tear the sky open. It went on and one, echoing off the hills and sending birds wheeling from the trees and spiralling skyward.

It stopped as suddenly as it had begun. Gerardo nodded grimly. "Now it is time to wait for the man Daltrey," he said. "Then our work will be finished."

Gerardo looked toward the brush as he spoke, and Lex instinctively followed the Apache's gaze as he climbed to his feet. Francisco appeared from the brush, followed by several of the former prisoners brandishing their knives and the uniforms of the two fugitives. Behind them came four more Apaches. In two pairs, each had the leg of one of the runaway soldiers. They dragged the corpses like so much rubbish. The dead men bounced over the rocks like ragdolls. Their bones cracked against the stones. Even at that distance, Lex could see the blood covering their naked bodies.

Francisco headed straight toward Lex. He was bleeding from a gash in his shoulder, but didn't seem fazed by it. Planting himself in front of Lex, he extended a hand. "Thank you for your help," he said. Turning to the young Apache, he said, "Gerardo, go back to the rim and watch for Juana's signal. They will be here soon."

Lex took the hand and shook it solemnly.

Francisco continued. "I will try to give you the man Wade Daltrey. But I can make no promises. My people are eager for revenge."

"So I see," Lex said.

"Maybe you should go," Francisco said.

Lex shook his head. "Not without the man I came for. Dead or alive."

"It will be dead, señor. That I can promise you."

FRANCISCO ORGANIZED the warriors, selecting those with the best Spanish to wear the uniforms stripped from the Mexican soldiers. Lex helped gather the rifles and pistols, making sure all were loaded and in good working order. He distributed ammunition and then deployed the uniformed Apaches in some semblance of military fashion.

Lex wasn't familiar with Mexican Army standards, but based on what he had seen, this particular unit didn't really have much in the way of standards to begin with. The nature of the assignment suggested it might have been used as a punishment detail. It certainly was punishment, whether intentional or not.

What he wanted was for the Apaches to look busy. If they seemed to have something to do, Daltrey would be less likely to suspect that anything was wrong. This time, all the women and the younger Apaches were herded into the mine shafts for their own protection. At Lex's suggestion, a small contingent of armed warriors without army uniforms was posted at the mouth of the shaft as a last line of defense.

Francisco had resisted the idea initially. He argued that the advantage of numbers now lay in his favor. But Lex had seen something Franciso had not. The weapons captured from the soldiers were old, probably unreliable, and definitely not anywhere near as efficient as the Winchester and Springfield carbines Daltrey and his men were carrying. Many of the captured rifles were single shot affairs, and even a marksman practiced in their use would be at a disadvantage against the rapid fire Daltrey's men could lay down. For the Indians who had never used them before, that disadvantage would be magnified but, Lex hoped, not to a fatal degree.

The plan called for entrapment, letting Daltrey and his men come all the way into the canyon before attempting to disarm them. Lex was worried, though, that the captives would be in danger and this was just the kind of advantage Daltrey would recognize and attempt to capitalize on.

Francisco kept pushing aside Lex's fears. "Our women and children have seen the best blue coats the white-eyes have sent against us. They are not afraid of guns. They are not afraid of dying."

"But you don't *want* them to die, if it can be avoided," Lex argued.

"No. But they will not. If we start shooting, they will know what to do. They will not be harmed. And we will not shoot carelessly. The weapons are unfamiliar to us, as you say. But we know how to hit what we shoot at, and we will not shoot at our own people."

"And what if Daltrey says *he* will shoot them, unless you lay down your guns? What then?"

"Then he will start to shoot them, because we will not lay down our guns. And in the end, we will kill them all. Even your man Daltrey, if that is how it has to be."

At first blush, it seemed needlessly callous, even brutal, but on reflection Lex realized that it was an approach that had been born and reared under the muzzle of white-eyes guns. There was no reason to give in to threats, because once you capitulated, if you were an Apache, the chances are your women and children were slaughtered anyway, and then you had no guns to protect them.

Lex took one last walk around the canyon, looking for anything at all that might tip Daltrey that something was amiss. But he saw nothing. As he was coming back to join Francisco at the canyon mouth, he had to pass the cauldron. He looked at it, feeling an idea trying to take shape in his mind, but before he had a chance, Gerardo shouted from the rimrock that he had seen Juana's signal.

As in the earlier combat, the Apaches had men stationed up on the canyon rim. Some of the better marksmen were among them. They had captured rifles, a few repeaters, but mostly single shots. Some, as Lex had seen, were British Enfields, reliable but heavy and unwieldy compared to the lighter and more versatile American carbines. The warriors on the rim had also collected a number of large rocks which they could push or hurl down into the canyon if Daltrey and his men attempted to take cover at the base of the walls. Since that was where the sparse available cover lay, it was likely the rocks would come in handy.

Other warriors, some of the freed slaves, who

were weak and poorly armed, were stationed outside the mouth of the canyon. Once Daltrey entered the canyon, they would close off the only escape route. In the open, Daltrey's men would be easy targets if they bolted back out of the box canyon.

The signal was to be sent as soon as Daltrey passed Juana's position, rather than on first sighting, so that the flash would not be visible coming from behind them. That also meant Francisco and his men would know exactly how far away the raiders were. Two miles. Fifteen or twenty minutes at the most.

Lex quickly threw up a wall of firewood in one corner, making a nest for himself. Ducking down behind the logs, he was still able to see the opening into the canyon, and he had plenty of cover. If he were charged, though, he would be boxed in. He crossed his fingers and hoped his Winchester wouldn't jam. Then held his breath and waited.

It seemed like an hour before the first distant clop of hooves could be heard. A horse nickered, and someone shouted, too far away to be understood. Across the canyon mouth, he could see Gerardo and Francisco. He glanced at the rim, looking for Benito, but saw no trace of him. Even though he knew roughly where the Apaches had concealed themselves, they were so well hidden, he could see nothing.

Lex could hear more horses now, their hooves pounding on the hard ground. The thunder swelled in the canyon, echoing off the walls. Several of the Apaches in uniform shifted nervously. They tried to look as if they were busy, but kept glancing over their shoulders toward the oncoming raiders.

Lex wondered whether Daltrey knew the officer in charge who, it turned out, had been a lieutenant. That could cause problems. As a former officer himself, Daltrey would doubtless go by the book. If the lieutenant weren't available, it might set off alarms in Daltrey's head.

The thunder grew louder now, filling the canyon. Lex tensed his grip on the Winchester, levered a shell home, and curled his finger around the trigger.

The first horses entered the canyon, riderless, and prancing skittishly. They headed straight for the palisade. The first two riders appeared. Neither one was Daltrey. They reined in, and nudged their mounts to one side to make room for the others.

Several more riderless horses followed them, chased after the others, and were trailed by more mounted men. They had rifles in their hands, as if they were uncertain what sort of reception to expect. Still, Wade Daltrey was nowhere to be seen.

The first of the prisoners stumbled in, three women, their knees bloody above the tops of their buckskin leggings. The sound of the hooves died away. Lex could hear the scrape of feet on the sandy ground, and the clop of a solitary set of hooves. It had to be Daltrey. He did a quick head count—thirteen. Daltrey would make fourteen.

"*Hola*?" The deep baritone of Wade Daltrey abruptly bounced off the canyon walls. As its echo died away, a thick silence descended on the canyon. The Apaches were watching the raiders, shifting their positions slightly, trying to get the best angle in the event it came to a gunfight.

Once more, Daltrey shouted. "*Hola*! "Diego, you there?"

Lex could see Daltrey's horse now, then the thick hands of the guerrilla chief as his horse walked slowly into the canyon. The sound of the hooves was hollow and deep, like stones falling into a well.

"Come on, dammit," Lex whispered. "Just a few more feet."

His palms were sweaty, and he wiped one hand on the legs of his pants, then the other. He could see Daltrey in profile now. The big man pushed his dusty hat back on the crown of his head, the brim jutting up at a sharp angle.

The horse stopped. Lex had him broadside, but there wasn't enough of an angle to really get the drop on him. Daltrey was suspicious. His horse danced sideways a step or two as Daltrey stood in the stirrups.

He shouted to the nereast man in uniform, "Where is Lieutenant Diego?"

The Apache at first shook his head, as if to signify that he spoke no English.

Lex couldn't wait any longer.

"All right, Daltrey," he shouted, getting to his feet behind the firewood barricade. "Drop your guns, all of you! You're surrounded. There's no way out."

Daltrey swiveled his head toward Lex. "You!" he said. "What the hell . . . ?"

And he went for his gun, backing his horse at the same instant.

The horse reared as Lex fired, but the animal was between Lex and his target. He saw the bullet strike the horse in the chest and the animal whinnied in pain. All hell broke loose in the same moment. Gunfire erupted from the riders, and the sharpshooters on the rimrock opened up a second later.

Daltrey leaped from the saddle and started to run back toward the mouth of the canyon.

The women screamed and tried to take cover, but were hampered by the ropes yoking them together. Instead, they gathered the children and covered them with their bodies as they fell to the ground.

Lex vaulted over the barricade as the canyon filled with the staccato rattle of gunfire. Bullets ricochted off the rock, spangling and whining as they bounced from wall to wall.

Several of the raiders, startled by the sudden fury, jumped from their saddles as their horses, terrified by the uproar, wouldn't hold still. Staying in the saddle meant they would be unable to aim accurately and they knew there were guns trained on them from every side.

Daltrey was already heading out of the canyon as Lex raced after him. The Ranger saw the big man disappear behind a chimney rock, and sprinted for the opening, hoping none of the Apaches mistook him for one of Daltrey's men.

War whoops cut through the gunfire, sharp howls and yelps shattering on the stone walls and cascading down into the canyon. Outside the canyon mouth, more gunfire broke out.

As Lex raced through the opening, he saw Daltrey fifty yards ahead, his long legs pumping as he charged straight for a pair of Apaches who were struggling with their unwieldy rifles. Daltrey shot one in the chest, then hurled himself to one side, narrowly avoiding the thrust of a bayonet.

He fired again, hitting the second Apache in the shoulder and knocking him down.

Lex dropped to one knee and fired, but Daltrey was zigzagging, and the shot went wide.

Getting to his feet again, Lex shouted, "You can't get away, Daltrey. Give it up!"

But the guerrilla raider ignored him. He didn't look back, and he didn't slow up. Behind him, Lex heard more shouts and gunfire. He turned to see three of Daltrey's men trying to fight their way out of the canyon as the Apaches in the rear guard swarmed out of the rocks and charged toward them, swinging their captured rifles overhead like warclubs.

Breaking into the brush along the creek, Daltrey disappeared from view again. Lex raced after him, conscious that Daltrey could easily lay in wait and pick him off from cover before he knew what had hit him.

He could still hear the big man floundering through the brush, then a splash, as Daltrey leaped into the water. Lex slowed, trying to hear whether Daltrey would cross the creek or continue on. Several more splashes suggested he was trying to run in the shallow water, free of the entangling brush and vines.

Lex took a calculated gamble. Rushing along the outer reaches of the brush, he followed the streambed for fifty yards. He could still hear Daltrey plodding through the current, and he knew he was gaining.

He ran another forty yards, and knew he'd passed Daltrey. The splashing stopped then, and Lex stopped running, waiting for Daltrey to make the next move. He knew the guerrilla chief might be listening for the sounds of his progress, trying to decide what his next step should be.

The gunfire from the canyon was strangely distant now. The war whoops of the Apaches still sliced through the air, but they were less frequent and more piercing, as if the battle had settled down into a war of attrition.

Lex had to make a decision, and he made it impulsively. Easing toward the brush, he started toward the creek, trying to push the branches aside as silently as possible. The splashing had not resumed, and he wondered whether Daltrey were laying in wait or had moved to the edge of the creek or on across and up into the rocks on the far side.

Lex could see the glitter of water through the brush now, and he dropped to the ground to wiggle the last few yards. Under the thickest of the growth, his progress was almost silent.

He could reach out and dip his fingers in the current now, he was so close. Craning his neck to look downstream, he saw no sign of Daltrey, but he decided to hold his ground. He was so damned close. There was no way on earth he was going to make a mistake now, not after what he'd been through. Patience, he thought, just have patience.

Breathing through his mouth, gulping air and holding it until he could no longer wait to let it go, he watched the bend in the creek. He still hadn't heard a sound from the guerrilla raider. The distant crackling of the guns in the canyon was gradually tapering off, and Lex was trying to decide whether it was a good sign or not, when he saw a stockinged foot twenty yards away.

Daltrey had taken off his boots and now stepped deliberately from stone to stone along the waterline. He was facing the other way, and Lex knew this was his best chance.

With a rush, he scambled to his feet and darted into the open.

"Drop it!"

Daltrey spun, slipped off a rock and landed feet first in the current, then landed on his butt with a loud splash, his arms flailing as he tried to keep from falling over on his side.

Daltrey's gun went off and the shot whistled just past Lex's ear. He charged forward, hoping to get to Daltrey before the man regained his balance, but Daltrey just sat in the creek, his thumb on the hammer of his Colt.

"What's all this to you?" he asked. "You don't give a damn about no Apaches."

"You wouldn't understand, Daltrey. Besides, it's not just about Apaches."

"I kind of liked you. Pity it has to end this way. For one of us."

"Drop it," Lex barked again, knowing as the words formed on his lips that he was wasting his breath.

Daltrey thumbed back the hammer and Lex fired.

The shot slammed into Daltrey's chest. He looked down at his shirt and fingered the bullet hole, already slick with blood. Trying to raise his pistol, he smiled distantly. Then Daltrey shook his head. The pistol in his hand rose slightly, then wavered. Lex fired again.

Daltrey slumped backward in the creek. His hat came off and spun around twice before the current caught it. It slid by quietly, dark patches free of dust where it had been immersed. The braid glittered brilliantly in the sun.

Lex watched for a moment, until it rounded a bend and disappeared.

LEX WALKED over to the body. He stood looking down at Daltrey's face, almost tranquil in repose. The thick black beard, just touched with gray at the temples, glistened with water. Daltrey's eyes were already glazed and they stared vacantly at the sky. Lex knelt beside the body, reaching into the water to take Daltrey's right arm by the wrist. He lifted it out of the water, heard the gurgle of water from the drenched sleeve, and felt for a pulse. The wrist was still. Wade Daltrey was dead.

For a moment, Lex wondered what strange twists and turns the man's life had taken. What, he wondered, makes a man go so desperately wrong? He looked up at the sky for a brief instant, but there was no answer in the clouds.

He let go of Daltrey's wrist. The limp arm splashed into the creek. Air bubbled out of the sleeve for a few seconds. Then there was silence, broken only by the babble of the current as it coursed among the stones.

For a moment, the silence seemed perfectly natural, almost appropriate. Then it struck him that the gunfire had stopped. He straightened and pushed through the brush, looking back at Daltrey one last time before letting the brush close behind him.

Struggling through the thick growth, he managed to get out into the open. He could see the mouth of the canyon now, nearly a quarter-mile away. He started to walk, then moved faster and faster until he broke into a run. Inside the yawning mouth of the canyon, Lex could see figures moving back and forth. Some still wore pieces of the Mexican uniforms, others the faded and dirty gray of the prisoners. In the broad, open expanse before the canyon, several bodies lay sprawled in the awkward indifference of death.

Smoke was starting to billow up toward the sky, but the canyon was strangely quiet. As he entered, he saw the Apaches tearing the last remnants of the palisade fence down, feeding it piecemeal to the fire next to the overturned cauldron. A puddle of corn gruel was already drying where it seeped into the ground next to the fire pit.

Lex looked for Francisco, but didn't spot him. Gerardo was helping to dismember one of the shacks against the wall, and Lex ran to him. He felt a hundred black eyes fixed on him, and his spine felt like it had frozen fast. Gerardo must have sensed his approach, because he turned when Lex was still several yards away.

He nodded, swept an arm widely to take in the carnage strewn around the canyon floor.

"See?" the Apache said. "You see?"

Lex nodded. "I see," he said. "Where are Benito and Francisco?"

Gerardo pointed toward the back wall of the

canyon. With the palisade down, Lex could see three yawning mouths gaping blackly at the base of the wall. In one corner, the waterfall cascaded from the rimrock and plummeted into a deep pool before wending its way along the canyon floor and out into the ravines beyond. A fine mist, spurred by a soft breeze, sifted out and down. It caught the sunlight and arced a graceful half rainbow across the rimrock high above.

But there was no sign of the Apache warriors. Suddenly, two figures appeared in the mouth of the middle mineshaft. They ran, shouting to the other Apaches, then dove to the ground. Lex felt the ground shake for a few seconds before he realized what was happening. Then a great rumble belched from the mineshaft, followed by a roiling cloud of dust.

Moments later, two more blasts shook the ground, and two more clouds of dust rolled out from the base of the wall. Francisco had blown up the shafts, sealing the mines with tons of fallen rock.

Lex nodded. It seemed somehow appropriate. He started to move toward the still prostrate Francisco and Benito. Gerardo reached for him, tried to hold him back, but Lex shook him off.

He reached the two warriors just as Francisco got up on his knees. Lex reached down, took him by the hand and tugged him to his feet. He did the same with Benito.

"The man Daltrey?" Francisco said.

"Dead."

"It is best," Francisco grunted. "You better go. It is not safe for any white-eyes here just now."

"I understand." He put out a hand and the Apache looked at it for a long moment, then grabbed it in his massive grip and shook it firmly.

Lex turned then and saw Juana on horseback, his chestnut and Dan Patterson's roan on a tether behind her. He waved and walked toward her. She leaned over to hand him the tether.

Lex took her hand in his own for a moment, then bowed, brought the hand to his lips and kissed it. He smiled then, and she seemed confused. Chuckling, he walked to the chestnut and swung into the saddle.

"Señor Cranshaw . . . ?"

It was Francisco. Lex nodded.

"Thank you," Francisco said.

"You be careful," Lex shouted.

Francisco smiled. "Here there are only Mexicans," he said. "But many stones."

Dan Mason is the pseudonym of a full-time writer who lives in upstate New York with his family.

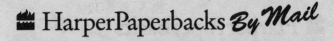
HarperPaperbacks *By Mail*

ZANE GREY CLASSICS

THE DUDE RANGER
0-06-100055-8 $3.50

THE LOST WAGON TRAIN
0-06-100064-7 $3.99

WILDFIRE
0-06-100081-7 $3.50

THE MAN OF THE FOREST
0-06-100082-5 $3.95

THE BORDER LEGION
0-06-100083-3 $3.95

SUNSET PASS
0-06-100084-1 $3.50

30,000 ON HOOF
0-06-100085-X $3.50

THE WANDERER OF THE WASTELAND
0-06-100092-2 $3.50

TWIN SOMBREROS
0-06-100101-5 $3.50

BOULDER DAM
0-06-100111-2 $3.50

THE TRAIL DRIVER
0-06-100154-6 $3.50

TO THE LAST MAN
0-06-100218-6 $3.50

THUNDER MOUNTAIN
0-06-100216-X $3.50

THE CODE OF THE WEST
0-06-100173-2 $3.50

ARIZONA AMES
0-06-100171-6 $3.50

ROGUE RIVER FEUD
0-06-100214-3 $3.95

THE THUNDERING HERD
0-06-100217-8 $3.95

HORSE HEAVEN HILL
0-06-100210-0 $3.95